Murder on the Downs

A Chance Inquiry Novel

HOLLY NEWMAN

CHAPTER 1

A PICNIC - MAY 1817

The pony cart lumbered up the hill.

"Is this safe?" queried Lady Cecilia Branstoke with a delighted laugh as the four-wheeled farm cart hit another bump in the narrow trail, which was little more than a sheep's path. The cart jerked to the left. She wrapped her right arm around her infant son while holding on to the edge of the cart with her other arm, swaying with the motion.

Since marrying Sir James two years ago, she'd been involved in multiple dangerous mysteries and had come to consider herself an intrepid individual, up for any adventure! And she still thought of herself as such; however, since the birth of their son five months ago, she found she had developed an air of caution she hadn't detected in herself before. The mother instinct, she supposed.

The pony cart driver—and instigator of a planned picnic—Lady Elinor Aldrich, laughed. "This is the worst, I promise you, and well worth the journey up the hill. Wait till you see the views!"

"I shall hold you to that," Cecilia returned as young Hugh whimpered at the cart's jostling.

Tied in place in the back of the pony cart and giggling with each bump rode one-year-old Charlotte, Elinor's daughter.

She'd met Elinor and her husband, Simon, Lord Aldrich, shortly after she and James had wed and moved into Summerworth Park. They had become fast friends, eschewing titles and addressing each other by their first names.

"Is this our destination?" Cecilia asked as they crested the hill onto a meadow covered with grasses and spring flowers swaying in the light, late morning breeze. She looked about. Though no trees grew within the meadow, stands of trees edged three sides except for where the road they'd come up from the west continued to cross the meadow and where the meadow slipped down to a valley in the east.

"Yes. We'll stop the cart at the edge of the wood. The horse will find plenty of chalk grass and wildflowers to graze upon."

Lady Elinor climbed down from the cart first and took Hugh from Cecilia's arms so she could easily climb down as well. After Cecilia shook out the skirt of her well-worn, comfortable blue muslin dress, she took Hugh back and looked again around the beautiful meadow. She could hear birdsong in the stands of trees and the breeze rustling the leaves like little bells. Cowslips and Bird's-foot trefoil clusters of yellow and orange dotted the meadow, and a white and blue little flower Cecilia couldn't name had sprinkled itself throughout the grass.

"Who told you about this place for a picnic?" Cecilia asked Elinor as she inhaled a sweet, honey-like scent from nearby flowers.

"Mrs. Jones," Elinor said absently as she untied the straps that held Charlotte in place.

"The Vicar's wife?"

"Yes, she likes to come here to practice her watercolor painting. But after she told me about it, I learned it is a well-known meadow for family outings, with the sheep grazing areas a little further down the road we came up." Elinor lifted Charlotte out of the cart and then handed her a pillow, telling her she could help Mama take things to their picnic spot.

"Mrs. Jones paints?" Cecilia asked. She couldn't envision the busy, stout, smiling, and gossipy woman sitting still long enough to paint.

Elinor gave her a side-eye glance with a wry smile as she handed Cecilia the Branstoke basket of picnic offerings. "If one would call it painting. The poor dear tries. I have offered to teach her what I know, and I know others have as well, but she has turned all offers aside. She simply enjoys doing the painting, whether it is good or not. —And I shouldn't imply she is that bad; I've seen improvement over time. Her dawn and dusk skies are not as muddy-colored as they were a year ago." She picked up a blanket and her basket. She led the way to a spot on the west edge of the meadow where a few ash trees stepped into the meadow, promising shade.

"If I were one to paint, I should imagine this would be a beautiful place to do so. But why don't the sheep graze here?" Cecilia asked as she followed Elinor.

"Because of the escarpment," Elinor said, pointing to the far side of the meadow where no trees grew. "Simon tells me sheep and lambs can be amazingly clumsy near a cliff edge," she said drily.

"I wouldn't have thought that of sheep," Cecilia mused.

"The real reason is the edge is where another band of chalk nears the surface of the land, and chalk can be crumbly and fall away underfoot. We shall stay to this side of the meadow."

"I should say so!"

Elinor spread the blanket out, and the women used their baskets of food to anchor opposite corners of the blanket against the occasional gusts of wind. They went back and forth to the cart a few times for other items.

"There, now that is done, it only needs our husbands, and we may eat," Elinor said.

"Where do you suppose the gentlemen are?" Cecilia asked. "I expected them to scout out a favored spot for us. I told James, since it isn't too hot today, that I wanted dappled sunlight."

"Most likely looking at sheep," Elinor said. "Simon has been wanting to show James his sheep. He wants to discuss combining resources," she said with a wry smile. "Charlotte and I will walk to the top of the road—such as it is—to see if we can see them in the valley beyond."

Cecilia nodded as she removed her straw bonnet. She lay back contentedly against a pillow as she held Hugh. She and Hugh were in the shade, except when the breeze gently blew the leaves of the trees above, allowing sunlight to flit across them. She watched as Elinor and Charlotte walked slowly to the crest of the hill to look down sloping hills into what Cecilia knew was the dry valley below. She saw Elinor raise her handkerchief in the air and wave it before she turned with Charlotte to come back to the picnic blanket. Elinor paused a moment when Charlotte stopped to pick a wildflower. The little girl, surprisingly stable on her chubby little legs, hurried toward Cecilia and held the flower out to her.

"Thank you, Charlotte!" Cecilia enthused. She made a show of sticking the flower in her hair. Charlotte laughed and awkwardly clapped her chubby little hands together.

"As I thought, they are looking at sheep," Elinor said as she sat down on the blanket. "They saw me and indicated they would join us." She reached across the blanket to grab Charlotte's hand before she could put a clump of grass in her mouth. "No, darling, we don't eat grass," she said as she pried the grass from her fingers.

Charlotte's features screwed up as if she were going to cry.

"That's food for the sheep. You mustn't steal their food," Elinor said patiently. "Let me get you a biscuit that Mrs. Wembly had Cook put in the basket specifically for you." She pulled the basket toward her to rummage inside as Charlotte excitedly cried, *"Kit, kit!"* while bouncing on her bum.

"I suppose that is what I have to look forward to," Cecilia said with a laugh.

"Worse, probably," Elinor exclaimed, teasing. "He's a boy! It will be bugs and rocks and dirt!" she said with dramatic horror.

Cecilia laughed. "No doubt. Ah. Here come our wayward gentlemen. James! I thought you were to stake out our picnic site."

"You are here sooner than we expected," James said with his characteristic laconic tone as he dismounted and tied his horse's reins to a willowy sapling that would allow the animal easy grazing in the area.

"Has Simon convinced you to invest in sheep?" Elinor

asked as she wiped biscuit crumbs off Charlotte's cheeks and chin.

"Nothing to convince, for I have been considering that course for some time, in addition to building an oast house."

"Oast house? You want to make beer?" Elinor asked.

"Possibly. The estate already has hop and barley crops."

Cecilia nodded. "With an oast house, we can dry our own hops and either make our own beer or package and sell barley and hops to brewers—or perhaps do both!"

Simon laughed. "When I told James that the villagers in the dry valley use sheep manure to fertilize their crops, his interest piqued."

Cecilia turned her head to look at her husband. "Surely, they don't cart the manure down to the fields."

"No. Aldrich tells me they let them forage on the hills during the day and bring them down into the valley at night so they might fertilize the fields, then return them to the hills the next day."

Cecilia frowned. "That seems like a great deal of effort."

"Aldrich suggests we share resources," James said as he leaned over to tickle his son's nose with a blade of grass. Hugh sneezed.

"That is what Elinor told me," Cecilia said, pushing his hand away. Now Hugh was blowing bubbles through his nose. She wiped his nose with her handkerchief.

James leaned back on his elbow and looked over at Aldrich. "Have you talked to Mortlake at all about this idea to share resources? It seems to me he might be interested as well."

Aldrich compressed his lips. "Not yet. I don't feel Mortlake senior would be interested in sheep, and they already have an oast house for Mortlake Brewery. He's more invested in rebuilding the family seat in Sussex, but that son of his, Viscount Kendell, is anxious to make his mark and see the property producing more."

"Really?"

Elinor shook her head. "James, you are forgetting the Mortlakes look down on us because I come from trade," she interjected.

"That is more Lady Mortlake," Cecilia said. "Her son is cut from a different cloth. He seems a fine young gentleman—very polite and solicitous on all the occasions I've met him. And his father, the Earl, seems to be a fair man."

Elinor shrugged. "Maybe. Charlotte, come back here!" Elinor called out to Charlotte who'd walked all of five steps away from her mother.

The other adults laughed. "She merely wants to explore her world," Simon said.

"And eat grass," Cecilia offered.

"I know, I know. I only worry about her so. Makes me wish I had eyes in the back of my head too! I want to get out the picnic things so we may enjoy lunch. I'm looking forward to your estate ale," Elinor told Cecilia and James. "Simon, would you follow after Charlotte for me, please? Do not let her out of your sight! Toddlers are quick when they want to be."

"I should be delighted to!" her husband said, sweeping Charlotte up in his arms and giving her a tiny toss in the air. The child giggled delightedly.

Simon set her down, and she ran a few steps away from him, then turned to look back.

"Oh, you want me to chase you?"

Charlotte giggled and ran ahead, and Simon pretended to run after her. Suddenly, Charlotte stopped and plopped on the ground to pick up something.

Her father squatted next to her. "What did you find, Charlotte?" he asked.

Charlotte picked up what looked like a brooch from the grass. She studied it carefully, then she waved it in front of her as if expecting it to make noise.

"You found jewelry," her father said. "May I see?" he asked, putting his hand out to her.

She shook her head and held the brooch closer to her dress. "Mine."

"They learn that word quickly enough, don't they?" James observed as he walked toward them.

Simon laughed. "Yes, they do. Please?" he asked, extending his hand to her.

She pouted and pushed the brooch down between her legs.

"What you need is a distraction," James suggested. He unhooked his pocket watch from the chain that kept it secure. "See this?" He showed Charlotte the watch. She reached out a hand to take it. He pulled it back, barely out of her reach. "Do you want to trade? The watch for the jewelry?" he asked, pointing to where she had put the brooch.

Charlotte's little face screwed up tight. Then she brought out the brooch and threw it toward James. He laughed lightly, but he handed her his watch.

"Are you sure you want to give that to her?" asked Simon.

"A deal is a deal. And it is not a valuable watch." He stood up as he studied the brooch. It was a carnelian cameo of two women dancing. The carving was well done, the color of the carnelian rich and dark. It was set in a simple gold rope-style bevel setting.

Simon picked up Charlotte, who held tight to James' watch. "It looks familiar," Simon observed.

"Bring it here," Cecilia suggested, holding out her hand. "Perhaps Elinor or I might recognize it."

James returned to where he'd been sitting on the blanket and handed the brooch to Cecilia.

"I do recognize it! Look, Elinor, it's Mrs. Jones' brooch! She wears it nearly every day," Cecilia said as she passed it to Elinor.

"Yes." Elinor came up beside Cecilia and gently rubbed her fingers over the raised relief. "I often see her trace a finger over the design when she is stressed, as it relaxes her," Elinor said with a relaxed, remembrance smile. "I asked her about the carving one time, as typically, cameos are of one person in profile. She said the dancing girls represented sisters."

Cecilia looked at it again closely. "Probably lost it during her last painting session," she said.

"Pity about the clasp being broken. That's likely how she lost it. I can take it to her tomorrow," James said, "as I promised the vicar I would consult with him on the upcoming church repairs." He took the brooch from Cecilia and tucked it in his waistcoat pocket before lowering himself to sit on the blanket again.

"Lunch is ready," Elinor said. "Looks like our respective cooks have filled our baskets. We shall not go hungry!" she said as she passed around a platter full of various meats and cheeses, followed by a basket of bread, while James poured them mugs of ale.

~

"Oʜ, I dare swear I ate far too much of your cook's delicious fare," Cecilia said when all that remained of the picnic food were crumbs.

Elinor wiped her daughter's face as the toddler swayed and her eyes drooped. Elinor laid her down in the shade. Charlotte tried to fuss but too quickly succumbed to sleep. The parents laughed.

"Charlotte has the right of it; a nap right now is in order," Simon said. "I'll lie down beside my little darling," he yawned.

Cecilia stood up. "I need a walk to counter all that food."

"I'll join you," Elinor said. "We'll let the men watch the children."

"Don't I get a say?" James teased.

"No," the women said together. Laughing, he raised his mug of ale in salute.

Cecilia and Elinor walked to the edge of the meadow where shade and sunlight played together through the trees.

"I wonder when Mrs. Jones was last up here?" Cecilia mused.

"She tries to come a couple of times a week when the weather is favorable," Elinor said. "I believe she has been up here several times recently."

"I can't see her walking up here."

Elinor laughed. "No, not at all. She has a one-person pony cart she drives, or sometimes she rides. But it is a peaceful place, and she has been terribly depressed since Georgia Inglewood died, you know."

"No, I didn't. I haven't seen her since the night of your dinner party," Cecilia said.

Elinor compressed her lips. "She took the young woman's death personally."

Cecilia looked at her inquiringly.

"Miss Inglewood was increasing," Elinor said softly, as if they were in a crowd with others around to hear.

"Oh dear," said Cecilia.

"Precisely. And she approached Mrs. Jones to help her get rid of the child."

"Why would she come to the vicar's wife, of all people?"

Elinor shrugged. "I have no idea, but she did, and Mrs. Jones said she couldn't help her. She tried to counsel the girl to tell her young man the truth, but she got angry with Mrs. Jones and launched all manner of nastiness at her. I only know this because she was so loud I could not help hearing part of the conversation through the open vicarage window as my maid and I walked the lane to the drygoods store. After the girl was done spewing vitriol at Mrs. Jones, she ran off. I went to see Mrs. Jones. She had her face in her hands and was silently crying. She told me all that had happened, not only the bits I'd heard. I consoled her until the vicar came home, then she got up and practically threw herself at the poor man, knocking him back against the wall."

"Gracious! And you saw this?"

"Yes, and you know our vicar is a slender fellow," Elinor said with a twinkle in her eye.

"Surprising she didn't knock him to the ground."

"Indeed."

"She didn't mention any of this during the dinner party two nights ago, though we all were rather subdued, as we'd recently heard the news of Georgia's passing. She was quite pleasant that night," Cecilia observed.

"She may be a bit of a gossip; however, as a vicar's wife, she understands what to gossip about and when to remain silent. She entreated me to silence over what I'd heard and learned, as I entreated my maid as well."

Cecilia nodded. "When the girl died, it was given out as she died of something to do with her gut...something called an *iliac passion*. Do you believe that is the truth?"

Elinor shrugged. "I don't know; however, I know Mrs. Jones feared the girl committed suicide, and if that were the verdict, she could not be buried in the family graveyard, or be prayed over."

"As Squire Inglewood is now our local magistrate, do you suppose he paid off the coroner to espouse his explanation?"

"I don't know, though what I do know is that Dr. Patterson was not allowed to see the body."

"How strange. *Elinor!* Charlotte's up!" Cecilia exclaimed, seeing Charlotte running across the other side of the meadow.

"Oh no! The escarpment is that way!" Elinor cried, running after her daughter.

Cecilia followed, veering slightly to the left in case the child did one of her lightning-fast swerves that way.

Luckily, Elinor caught her daughter before she reached the cliff. Charlotte thought it was great fun and giggled and squealed with delight at the *catch-me* game.

Out of breath, Elinor sank to the ground, holding tightly to her happy child.

Cecilia let her breath expel. She smiled at her friend and her daughter. On the picnic blanket, Hugh was stirring. It wouldn't be long before she, too, was as worried for her child as Elinor, she mused as she watched James pick up Hugh and walk toward her, no doubt to change his nappy.

He handed the fussy baby to her.

Suddenly, he stepped closer to the escarpment, then turned toward Cecilia. "Take Hugh back to the blanket," he said, his tone low and urgent.

"What?" she asked, startled by her husband's change in manner.

He did not answer her; instead, he turned toward the picnic area. "Simon! Simon," he yelled.

Cecilia turned to look down the escarpment to see what had suddenly caught James' attention. Gleaming white chalk bands showed through bits of grass and shrubs in a near-vertical descent to the shallow valley some sixty feet below. A dangerous place for anyone to get too near, as attested by the sad, crumpled body of Mrs. Jones lying on a ledge more than halfway down the cliff.

CHAPTER 2

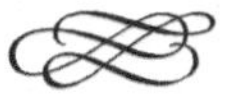

THE DOWNS

Simon rode down the hill on the sheep path Elinor and Cecilia had followed up to the meadow. He went to fetch Squire Inglewood, the magistrate, and Dr. Patterson on the extremely slim hope—voiced by his wife—that Mrs. Jones somehow remained alive.

James stayed by the cliff, studying the area for a way to descend to the bottom.

The women attended to the needs of their children, then hurriedly packed up the picnic and the pony cart. Neither talking, both women caught up in their thoughts of Mrs. Jones.

Charlotte looked tired again, so Elinor settled her lying down in the back of the cart, and Cecilia laid Hugh beside her. Hopefully, both children would sleep until they could take them home; otherwise, the rough trail could produce cranky children.

Cecilia couldn't stop thinking about the broken cameo brooch. Charlotte had found it on the other side of the meadow from the escarpment where Mrs. Jones had fallen.

If it had been a fall.

She pushed that thought ruthlessly out of her mind. Unfortunately, she had been involved in investigating too many murders over the past two years, since she'd met and married Sir James. She did not need another murder so close to home. And, unlike Elinor, she did not hold out the hope that Mrs. Jones yet lived. She would wait with the others for the magistrate and the doctor to arrive. Time enough for answers.

And yet that part of her drawn to mysteries couldn't help but wonder...

Had Mrs. Jones come to the meadow alone? If she had, where was her little pony cart and horse? Or had she ridden up, and if so, where was her horse? What had made Mrs. Jones cross from one side of the meadow to the other? Cecilia supposed she could have been searching out the best location for her painting. What time had she come? Had it been dark? Surely not. Who would have been here in the night? Unless they had been hoping to catch sight of fairies dancing in the meadow, she thought sardonically. If it weren't for the seriousness of the situation, she'd be tempted to dance across the meadow herself, for the wind carried the scent of the wildflowers that danced and swayed before the breeze. The leaves —nature's chimes—mingled with the songs of birds in the woods. So still, so blessedly normal. Everything about the meadow appeared beautiful and peaceful—if one did not look over the steep cliff edge along the southeast extent of the downs, as James now did.

She saw him sit down on a rock that rose out of the edge of the meadow. He took off one boot, then started to take off the other as Cecilia ran toward him.

"James! What are you doing?"

~

JAMES LOOKED up to see his wife running toward him. "I see a way to safely climb down the cliff to where she is," he said in his typical unemotional tone, which he'd mastered in the midst of chaos during the Peninsular War. Rising to his stockinged feet, he removed his jacket and handed it to Cecilia.

He could tell Cecilia wanted to protest, but she knew him too well to do so. Her pale pink lips compressed to a thin line. "Best wear your leather riding gloves" was all she said, digging them out of his jacket pocket and holding them out to him.

James saw the fear in her eyes, and his lips curled into a gentle smile. He leaned in to give her a kiss as he took the proffered gloves. "You are ever my treasure," he murmured.

Her lips quirked at the corners for all that remained unsaid.

He walked over to the edge of the cliff and squatted near the edge, studying the cliff face. Satisfied as to the best location to work his way down, he rolled up his sleeves, then turned around and carefully eased over the edge, his stockinged feet catching on clumps of dirt and occasional rocks. He would come down a few feet to the left of where Mrs. Jones lay, but believed he could make his way over to her.

He saw Cecilia step closer to the cliff to watch him. "Stay away from the edge, Cecilia. No telling what area might give way next," he said to her before turning his attention away from her and to the dangers of his descent.

Chalk rubbed against him, pieces breaking off to roll down the cliff face or to deposit streaks of the fine white dust upon his person. Soon, his eyes scratched, and grit filled his mouth and nose. He didn't know which felt worse, breathing through his mouth or his nose.

With each handhold and foothold he secured, he felt his body slide to the next.

His right foot slipped off its toehold, his leather-clad fingertips clinging tight to their holds, his arms aching with the strain of holding his own weight. The feeling reminded him of the horror of the Battle of Badajoz.

His toes finally found another ledge, this time a jutting rock he could trust. He pushed against it as his arms found closer handholds and his left foot followed to the small ledge that had halted Mrs. Jones' fall.

He relaxed slightly, allowing himself to take a deep breath. He was now even with Mrs. Jones. He worked his way slowly left toward her.

He glanced down into the ravine below. She'd landed on the narrow ledge on a small bit of rocks and chalk where chalk grasses grew in clumps. The clumps of grasses held the cliffside in place, while another ten to fifteen feet extended the drop to the bottom of the cliff.

James eased his way closer, finding a spot on the narrow outcropping that would support him without his hanging on the wall. He used his teeth to aid in removing his leather glove on his left hand. He reached over to gently touch her neck. A faint, fluttering beat surprised him.

She was alive!

"Mrs. Jones," he said urgently. "Can you hear me?"

There was a quiet moan from the woman.

James felt his heart begin to race as her eyes fluttered open to slits. Her fingers curled into claws, catching at the sleeve of his shirt. Her tongue slightly touched her lips. "Wa...wa..."

Water. Of course.

"Cecilia," he called out. "Cecilia!"

"Here, James," said Cecilia, peering over the cliff edge.

"Find a way to lower a pouch of water to me. She's alive!"

"Alive! How—?" she broke off. "Yes. Right away," she said instead, turning to run toward the wagon.

"Cecilia is getting you water," he assured Mrs. Jones as he heard Cecilia call out the good news to Elinor.

Mrs. Jones' eyes closed, her breathing ragged. James couldn't see how she could be alive. Her body lay twisted in an unnatural position. She must have multiple broken bones, and she must have been down here for hours.

A few minutes later, Cecilia lowered one of the picnic baskets, using a rein from the pony cart as a rope. Inside were a water pouch and some linen bandages. He dribbled some of the water on her parched, chalk-covered lips. Her tongue darted out to taste it. But the effort appeared too difficult, and she stopped. "No..." she exhaled. Her eyes opened again, more this time. They were a dull gray. She blinked, her fingers tightened on his shirtsleeve. "No pen...ny roy... Sto...p." Her chest heaved in her agitation. "Sto..." Her eyes closed, her body collapsing in on itself, her fingers loosening their hold, her hand falling away from his arm.

Dark memories of the condition of his men lying in surgeons' tents in Spain drew his brows together. As with them, James didn't imagine Mrs. Jones would live much longer, her body giving up. But James didn't give up.

He continued to talk to her softly, telling her Lord Aldrich had gone for help, to stay with him. There was no response from her, but he continued.

Her breathing changed to gulping air, a fish out of water. His heart clenched, for he recognized the death rattle, the herald of death to come. He turned his head and laid his forehead against the cliff. The sound was too much like Spain. He would live with those final sounds his whole life. For all his phlegmatic attitude within society, the sound haunted him.

CECILIA HAD ENJOYED her life in Kent with James and their son. She knew they should soon have to make the duty visits to his far-flung family, particularly his parents in Yorkshire and his cousin in Devon. And, of course, to her grandparents in Somerset. But in this spring air, she had reveled in being home. A cozy Georgian manor house, Summerworth Park suited her and James. It did not sprawl across the land as many aristocratic manor houses did. And thankfully, that was the case, for the old home had been long neglected and needed renovations. They were nearly finished with the house and were now turning their attention to other parts of the estate.

Cecilia no longer wanted mysteries and emotional upheavals now that they'd tasted a calm, everyday life. She had thought the village of Mertonhaugh would be free of such things. She sighed. She now wryly considered that naïve thinking on her part—or perhaps merely wistful thinking, people being people, good and bad, the world over.

She turned her head toward the trail when she heard the clomp of horse hooves and the creak of a wagon approaching.

To her surprise, when the wagon topped the rise, she recognized the brewer's wagon. On the seat next to the brewer on the driver's plank seat sat Dr. Patterson, and behind them rode Simon and Squire Inglewood, the magistrate.

Simon had made good time. He was back considerably before they thought he would be.

Waking to the sound of the wagon and the horses, Charlotte tried to climb out of the cart, but the sides were too tall for her chubby legs. She fell back on Hugh, startling him. He cried out, and startled birds flew up out of the nearby trees.

Cecilia swiped tears from her cheeks, then she picked Hugh up. Charlotte stood in the cart, her arms raised above her head and her little hands opening and closing as she demonstrated she wanted to be picked up too. Elinor pulled her out of the cart.

"I wish she could have slept longer. She's going to want to follow her father and the other men to look over the cliff," Elinor said, sniffling as she turned Charlotte away from the men's activities.

"We should take the children home and let the men do as they must," Cecilia suggested sadly.

"What? You have no curiosity!" Even through her sadness, Elinor gently prodded Cecilia for her friend's questing mind that had her investigating other mysteries.

"I do have curiosity, an abundance of curiosity; however, it doesn't serve me or Mrs. Jones at the moment. That's why I was suggesting we should take the children home," she sadly explained.

"Ah, your history had me worried about you for a moment," said Elinor with a sad, melancholy smile. "Unfortunately, their wagon blocks our way."

"That is easy enough to solve," Cecilia stoutly said. She laid Hugh back in the wagon and handed him the new bottle she and Hugh's nursemaid had picked out from the London circular on the marvelous new design of infant bottles to supplement nursing. Thankfully, he accepted it eagerly. She walked toward the men.

They were facing away, looking toward the cliff where her husband, covered in white chalk, was pulling himself up and over the top of the cliff.

"She's not dead," James told them.

"Not dead!" exclaimed the magistrate.

"Not yet," James said sadly. He turned to look at Dr. Patterson. "She has the death rattle breathing." He closed his eyes for a moment. "I doubt she'll survive our bringing her up," he said quietly.

Cecilia, seeing her husband's pain, pushed past the men to go to him and throw her arms around him.

Sir James stilled for a moment, then wrapped his arms around her, holding her tight.

Squire Inglewood, the magistrate, scowled at her. "Lady Branstoke, you should not come closer. This is not for a gentlewoman to see."

Cecilia nodded her head and stepped away from James. It was time for her playacting. She looked at the magistrate with wide blue eyes as she twisted her hands together. "I should never so impose, my lord. That would prove too upsetting, I am certain. Truly, I am fearful for when you bring poor Mrs. Jones up that I should turn sickly. When I heard what my dear Sir James said, I became so distraught I solely needed a hug of comfort," she said plaintively.

Out of the corner of her eye, she saw her husband raise an

eyebrow. He had been well aware of her helpless playacting since they'd met. And it was a role she'd adapted—at one time or another—in each of the mysteries they'd solved. Since she looked like a fragile woman, gentlemen did not see beyond her outward act to her cunning intelligence.

"Lady Aldrich and I should like to take the children home in her pony cart," she continued. "Unfortunately, your wagon blocks the way. Can one of you gentlemen move your wagon further into the meadow so we might go home?" she asked, looking from one man to another, a sorrowful, pleading look on her face. "I really cannot bear the thought of seeing Mrs. Jones in pain—or in death!"

Cecilia saw Sir James compress his lips against a knowing smile for her manner, instead maintaining his legendary sangfroid. The only man in the group to appear surprised by her manner was Dr. Patterson; none of the others knew her well enough.

"My apologies, milady," said the brewer, Mr. Haydon Vernon. He took his hat from his head. "My mistake. I shall move it immediately," he said, bobbing his head. Then he slapped his hat back on and fairly trotted over to his wagon, jumping into the seat with surprising agility for a man his size. He unwrapped the reins and encouraged his horse to move forward.

Cecilia waved her thanks to him, then hurried back to the cart.

Elinor shook her head. "I don't believe sugar melts in your mouth; you are entirely too sweet already," she said.

"Did I overdo it?" Cecilia asked, bending over the side of the wagon to see that Hugh still had the bottle in his chubby hands.

"I don't believe so, but I swear you should tread the boards," Elinor answered as she struggled to strap down a squirming child in the back of the wagon. "Stop it, Charlotte. We have to go home now so the men can work."

"No!"

"Yes. Cook should have tea biscuits ready for us by the time we get home. Don't you want more of those?"

"Kit!" Charlotte said. She began bouncing up and down. "Kit! Kit"

"Yes, a biscuit when we get home," Elinor said while she firmly tied Charlotte in place.

She turned to Cecilia. "Let me hold Hugh for you while you climb up on the cart, and I'll hand him to you."

Quickly, they were ready to leave.

Cecilia looked around the meadow and the rutted path off the hill with different eyes. Coming up, she saw the beauty and simplicity of nature. Now she looked for any irregularities—trampled grasses, a dropped item, evidence of a snagged coat, anything that might indicate another person had been on the downs with Mrs. Jones, and who they might be. But the road and its surroundings were as clean and beautiful as she recalled them being that morning. One would think death would leave markers.

Unfortunately, it seldom did.

She positioned Hugh higher against her chest. She certainly hadn't been looking for another mystery, but she couldn't ignore this one. She liked Vicar Jones and his wife. They were good people and were good for the community. It behooved her and James to uncover the truth of Mrs. Jones's fall off the cliff. It was the least she could do for that kind, jovial woman.

"Elinor, I didn't see any sign of Mrs. Jones' pony cart, did you?"

"No, but she has a smaller, two-wheeled cart; I suppose her horse could have wandered off with it, looking for more grass."

"Hmm, possibly, if she hadn't set the brake properly, I suppose. But if she drove or rode her horse, would the horse have gone far?"

Elinor shook her head. "No, and the horse she uses is old Milton, retired from years of being Lady Mortlake's mount."

"How is it you know all these small details?" Cecilia asked.

Elinor laughed ruefully. "From Mrs. Jones. She didn't like how Simon and I were excluded from Mertonhaugh's small society due to my middle-class antecedents, so she strived to visit me frequently. And that woman can talk. Sometimes, her visits could get overwhelming; however, I saw they served a purpose for her, though I never sussed out what that service might be. And she has been like a grandmother to Charlotte since neither my nor Simon's mother yet lives. She often came over on the day she knew the nursemaid had off and took it upon herself to care for Charlotte."

"Did she ever have children of her own?" Cecilia asked.

"You know, I don't know, but I suspect she did but never spoke on that, and I didn't ask for fear that was a painful tale."

Cecilia nodded, then sighed. "Do you think…do you think she might have taken her life by jumping off that cliff?" she asked tentatively, mindful of the close relationship Elinor had had with Mrs. Jones.

"No. That would never enter my mind. She was too full of life."

"But what about that circumstance with Georgia Inglewood? Could she have somehow felt guilty for Georgia's death?"

Elinor paused for a moment before answering. "No. She believed—or chose to believe—the verdict of an *iliac passion*—in common terms, a ruptured appendix."

"I take it you do not believe she died of a ruptured appendix?"

"Not when I discovered they refused Dr. Patterson access to her body and she was buried quickly."

"You feel she committed suicide and her family hid that fact, and was able to do so since he is the magistrate?"

"I hate to say this; however, they are so starchy, I wouldn't put it past them... But I don't know, and I should hate to be accounted spreading heedless gossip, you know how gossip can get a life of its own!"

"Indeed, I do. I have experienced that. It is also what has helped me to maintain the myth that I am a fragile woman. People hold on to gossip harder than what they might see."

Elinor laughed. "Too true," she said as she pulled up the cart before Summerworth Park, surprised Charlotte remained asleep.

Daniel, one of their senior footmen, quickly came out the front door. They signaled him to be quiet, and the young man grinned and nodded. He helped Cecilia and Hugh to the ground.

"I'll retrieve our picnic items from you later," Cecilia whispered to Elinor, for she didn't want to wake the baby.

Elinor nodded and drove on toward her home.

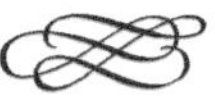

CHAPTER 3

The widowed Mrs. Threadmont met Cecilia in the upstairs hall. "Let me take him, ma'am." The young woman reached to take Hugh from Cecilia's arms. Hugh fussed. "Hush, hush, little one. Let's not wake my Ronnie. I'll get you cleaned up and fed in a trice," the woman cooed.

Cecilia smiled at Hugh in Mary Alice Threadmont's arms. "Thank you, Mary Alice," she said. "He did take from that new bottle we ordered, so he has had something to eat, but it has been a while." She was grateful to have Mary Alice Thread-mont as Hugh's nursemaid and sometimes wet nurse. That she had experienced widowhood soon after her own babe had been born was a distressing circumstance. However, it allowed her to take the wet nurse position with the Branstokes.

Her late husband had been a tenant farmer on the Aldrich estate when he'd been kicked in the head by one of the horses, only to fall backward against another horse who reared up and trampled him beneath its hooves. It had been a heart-wrenching accident for all who witnessed the incident and for those who had not but knew the man to be an honest, hard-working, devoted husband to his young wife.

Though the Aldriches had promised her a pension on behalf of her late husband, Mary Alice preferred to work and had approached Cecilia with the offer of her services when her child was born. Cecilia quickly agreed and had Mary Alice and her young son move into Summerworth Park to acclimatize themselves to the household and its routine. In the five months since Hugh had been born, she had proved a treasure to Cecilia.

Cecilia followed the widow into Hugh's nursery and watched her prepare to give Hugh a bath. "Mary Alice," Cecilia said as she watched her pull his small arm out of his garment, "did you know Mrs. Jones well?"

Cecilia had liked Mrs. Jones, but, in light of her death, she wondered how well she had really known her and was curious as to the opinions of others.

"Know her well?" Mary Alice shrugged. "I suppose as well as a body could know the vicar's wife. She is always good to me and wouldn't hear no gossipy untruths that said my Ronnie did not die, as reported in the inquest."

"People would do that?"

"Lord love ya, ma'am, yes. Nothing the village likes more'n is imagin'n the worst, like they done with the Baron and Lady Aldrich." Her eyes narrowed. "And I could tell you the worst tale-bearers, too… Why do you ask about Mrs. Jones?" she asked as she turned toward Hugh.

Cecilia inhaled deeply. "The woman is dying—she might already be dead," she said, her voice low. It seemed unreal to speak of her as dead. She felt her throat tighten and her eyes burn again, as they had on the meadow.

Mary Alice whipped around to face Cecilia. "Dead!" she exclaimed, her face white as a sheet. "What? How?"

"We saw her down the escarpment." Her face grew pinched. "Her body lay on a small ledge, contorted in a most unnatural manner."

Mary Alice looked at her numbly. Hugh, forgotten, rolled on his side. Cecilia stepped up to her son, laying a steadying hand on him. With her other hand, she gently guided Mary Alice to sit in the chair by the table.

"I'm sorry. Perhaps I shouldn't have told you—at least at the moment—but I fear it will become common knowledge before nightfall."

Mary Alice nodded weakly, tears rolling down her cheeks. "Y-y-yes," she said slowly, her voice broken. Then, she looked up at Cecilia and cleared her throat. "Yes, it will," she said again, stronger. She ran her tongue across her lips. "I am glad I come to hear of it from you... You say she is dying, but might be dead now? How?" she finally asked into the silence between them.

Cecilia shrugged. "We don't know yet." She picked her son up, burying her face against his neck. She needed the touch of his young life to shore up the agony of another's death. "That is up to the doctor and the coroner when she dies, I presume. Sir James said she was near death. She could have been pushed, or—I suppose—it might be a suicide."

"Mrs. Jones? Commit suicide?" The idea of suicide drew Mary Alice out of her temporary shock. "No, no, I hardly think so, milady," she argued. "That would not be what Mrs. Jones would do."

"There will be plenty to imagine such, for we saw no sign

of her pony cart or horse on the meadow, but we did find her favorite brooch."

"The one with the dancing girls on it?" Mary Alice asked.

"Yes. It was on the other side of the meadow in the tall grasses, the clasp broken."

"The other side? Do you suppose she could have been looking for it and got too close to the edge?"

"And the ground gave way beneath her?" suggested Cecilia.

"Yes."

Cecilia considered that possibility and nodded. "That might make more sense than someone pushing her, or her throwing herself off the cliff. Both my husband and Lady Aldrich did warn me that the edge was known to be crumbly. I'm sure the men who came to get her body will consider that factor as well."

Mary Alice gathered herself together and busied herself about the room. She handed Cecilia a clean gown for Hugh.

"Thank you." Cecilia slipped the gown over Hugh's head and pulled the garment down. "Are you all right now to take Hugh for a while?" Doubt colored her voice.

"Yes, ma'am," said Mary Alice, as crisply as she might. She began loosening the top of her gown so she could put Hugh to her breast.

"I'll take Hugh for the night," Cecilia told her as she watched her hungry son suckle. "However, I would appreciate your taking him all day tomorrow, I believe I shall be busy talking to people about Mrs. Jones and her death."

"Yes, ma'am. I can do so… I can't help thinking about her brooch." She stroked the fine hair on Hugh's head. "You know it represents her daughters?"

"Her daughters! I wasn't aware she had daughters," Cecilia said, sitting down on the daybed in the room.

Mary Alice nodded slowly. "Yes. Twins. Faith and Hope. They're a mite older'n me. I didn't know them well—none of us did, as the vicar and Mrs. Jones sent them to a lady school."

"You mean like a finishing school?"

"I guess. I asked Miss Faith about it when they come back from their schoolin'. She said it was so they could marry up, but she said it with a laugh like that were a funny notion. They weren't here long afore they left. Don't know where they went or what jobs they mighta got."

"They will need to be notified. When I speak with the vicar tomorrow, I'll see what we can do to get them here in a timely fashion. They may need a letter to their employers to verify the need." Cecilia stood up. "Thank you for telling me about Mrs. Jones' daughters."

"Acorse, milady. And I be seein' you tomorrow. Early like."

CECILIA WAITED in the morning room for James to return home, curled up on the couch with her rust-colored tabby cat, Randy, in her lap. The animal seemed to sense Cecilia's disquiet and purred quietly, bunting her hand for her to pet him. Cecilia did as the cat requested and found her disquiet ease with the calming, petting motion, though she couldn't stop thinking about Mrs. Jones and the vicar.–And the fact they had two daughters!

What would that poor man do without his wife to keep him smiling, for Cecilia knew she had.

After her discussion with Mary Alice, she knew there was

much she didn't know about the vicar's wife. Two daughters! She'd never mentioned them—nor, interestingly, had anyone else. In a village as gossipy and full of tales as Mertonhaugh, how could that be? How were the vicar and his wife able to send them to a finishing school? That was not typically within the stipend of a vicar. Perhaps Mrs. Jones had had money, or another relative had and wished to see benefits bestowed upon the girls. Better in many ways than simply funding dowries.

The daughters were no longer in the area. Where did they go? Were they married now, or did they leave to discover work? She hoped not to London. That was a rough place for two young women from the country to find their way. Too many who went to the city found themselves caught up in the bawdy houses, gambling dens, or simply reduced to begging on the streets.

She paused and laughed humorously at herself for her racing mind. She did not have James' ability to take all bits of information in stride; instead, she must dissect each bit of knowledge and play with it.

She sighed and rang for Coggins.

"Yes, milady?" he asked from the doorway.

"Could you please light the lamps and close the drapes? I hadn't realized the lateness of the hour. Ask Cook to hold dinner, please, and in the meantime, as we await James, please bring me a sherry.—Actually, bring the tray with extra glasses...and brandy as well. Sir James may prefer that after his afternoon activities."

Coggins nodded. "Of course, milady. As you say."

Cecilia could tell by his solemn, heavy-eyed expression

that the news about Mrs. Jones, and where Sir James was, had spread through the household.

COGGINS HAD BARELY handed Cecilia her sherry when they heard a commotion in the front hall.

James was home.

"Quickly, Coggins, have him come in here before he goes upstairs to clean up," Cecilia said.

Coggins did as she asked, and in another moment, James stood in the morning room doorway. Covered in white chalk dust, he resembled a ghostly shade more than a man.

"Cecilia, love, I am in all my dirt," he said tiredly. "Can't I tell you everything after I've changed?"

"Yes, you can; however, first…brandy. You deserve it," she said, rising from her seat on the sofa, much to her cat's meowed dismay. She poured James a glass of brandy, then took it over to him.

"She spoke to me," James revealed tiredly.

"She did?" Cecilia's eyes widened. She'd known she'd been alive, but she hadn't realized Mrs. Jones had had any moments of communication.

"Yes. It wasn't much, and I'm certain our magistrate will make a hash of it," James said.

"You haven't told him yet?"

"There wasn't the opportunity with him taking command as he did. We were his enlisted soldiers, told what to do and basically ordered not to speak or think."

Cecilia laid a hand on James's arm. "What did she say?"

He took another sip of his brandy before answering. "She said *no* and then *pennyroyal*, then *stop*, and she was quite agitated when she said *stop*." He paused and looked across the room, like he was visualizing again what had happened. He turned back toward Cecilia. "That effort, I feel, is what took her to the edge. She fell into unconsciousness. She passed soon after, before Dr. Patterson scaled down the cliff face to examine her. ...I confess, my love, my realization of her life, followed so swiftly by her death, hit me hard, as it reminded me too vividly of my men dying in Spain," he confessed. He handed her back the brandy glass as his head dropped down to his chest..

"My dear heart," she said. She reached up to lay a hand on his pale, dirt-streaked face. "Thank you for seeing to Mrs. Jones during her last moments. I'm sure it gave her comfort not to be alone. Wait a moment, and I'll pour you another glass of brandy to take upstairs."

He clasped his hand around hers and held it against his cheek, then moved it to his mouth and kissed her palm. She sighed at his attentiveness. She saw him sigh deeply when he dropped her hand.

"Tomorrow's inquest should prove interesting," he said in a sad, pained manner.

Cecilia's heart went out to him for what he'd been through to be with Mrs. Jones, and with the memories it evoked. "You look so tired," she said. "Would you like to forego the dining room tonight and have a dinner tray in your chambers?"

"Will you join me?" he asked, looking at her fully, his dark eyes clouded with pain.

She smiled slightly. He was ever so steadfast, so phlegmatic. It hurt her soul to see him brought down now. "You get your bath while I get Hugh settled for the night, then I consider dining privately together to be an admirable idea."

CHAPTER 4

THE VICAR'S SORROWS

Sir James pulled up the phaeton in front of the rectory, then went around to assist Cecilia to descend. She briskly walked to the painted door to knock. She waited, but no one answered. She rapped again as Sir James walked to the right side of the house to look in a window. He looked back at her and shrugged. Cecilia walked to the other side of the house. She stopped, smiled, then waved James over.

The left side of the house boasted the rectory garden, which included a small, near-ground-level herb maze. The vicar stood in the middle of his wife's beloved low-lying garden maze, looking helplessly at the plants.

"Mr. Jones!" Cecilia called out.

He turned, nodded, and raised an arm in greeting, then he bent down to pluck a sprig of mint from the center of the maze.

Cecilia walked to the little garden, her husband coming up behind her.

"Mrs. Jones was always fussing with this mint," the vicar said, rolling the sprig of mint between his fingers. "Said it was a naughty plant that would try to take over her entire garden if she didn't keep it tended to its space." He smelled the plucked mint, then tossed it back on the ground.

"I don't know much about the other plants, I'm afraid. Regretfully, I didn't listen closely when she talked of her herbs. They were her babies and her passion—along with her painting."

He moved on to touch another delicate plant, studying it, as if this were the first time he had seen it. "Her painting surprised me. Started that two years ago when a painting set was sent to the grocer by mistake. When Mrs. Sandiford didn't know what she was going to do with it, my Miranda said she'd buy it from her. Said it might be fun. For months, she painted everything around here." He laughed tightly. "Soon, she was spending all her pin money on paints, brushes, and special paper. She was like a young girl, giggling at capturing some image entirely as she liked it, pouting when the picture she had envisioned didn't come together like it ought."

He stood up and brushed his hands together to wipe off stray pieces of plants and dirt. "Then one day she ventured to the meadow up there," he said with a jerk of his head in the direction of the cart track that led out of the village and up the hill to the meadow. "She loved the meadow for all the bits and pieces of nature she found to paint, and for all the changes each hour of the day brought."

Cecilia allowed her gaze to follow where he pointed, then turned back to the vicar. "Lady Aldrich told me sometimes she drove the pony cart up the hill and other times she rode a horse. What did she do the day before yesterday?"

"Rode. The cart was here when I got home, and last night, the horse she rides turned up back at the Mortlake stables."

"The Mortlake stables? Why there?" Cecilia asked.

"We acquired the horse from them. The horse was too old, and they were thinking to put the creature down. My Miranda would have none of that and asked if she might have him. He was a sorry lot when she first got him, but under her care, he grew strong enough for her to ride him and pull her little cart."

He sighed and looked intently at Cecilia. "She did so much, my Miranda. Always saw to the folks in need, saw to me to make sure my life was comfortable, saw to her garden and the animals here. It was a wonder she had any time to do everything, but she did, and always with a twinkle in her eye."

"I wanted to talk to you today, before it comes up at the inquest this afternoon," James said.

The vicar looked at him for a long moment. "Something about my Miranda and her death?" he asked, voice quavering.

James nodded. "After we saw her, and Lord Aldrich rode down to the village to contact the magistrate, I found a way to climb down the cliff to get to her."

The vicar blinked. "She was alive?" he asked on a threaded whisper. His face grew gray and haunted.

"Yes, but near death. She appeared badly hurt, I believed she had multiple bones broken—as the doctor attested when we pulled her off the ledge—and it looked like she'd bled out from a head wound. I touched her neck to see if I could feel her pulse. It was light and fluttering, but suddenly her fingers grabbed my shirt sleeve, and her eyes fluttered open. She whispered she needed water, her lips white from chalk dust."

"I sent some down to James as fast as I could," interjected Cecilia.

"I got some water in her, not much, but enough to, unfortunately, give her more awareness of her pain and where she was. I think she knew she was dying. Her fingers tightened on my sleeve. She said haltingly and so softly I could scarcely hear her, '*No. Penny. Royal. Stop. Stop.*' Do you have any idea why she might have said that?"

The vicar slowly shook his head. "She used to grow pennyroyal but stopped growing that about eighteen months ago."

James nodded, his lips compressed in a tight line. "Saying those words seemed to take the last of her strength. She then passed out, and a while later, I heard her death rattle begin. It brought back too many memories of my days in Spain."

The vicar reached out to James. "I'm sorry, but I am happy she was not alone at the end."

"Pennyroyal?" Cecilia repeated.

The vicar turned to her. "Yes."

"So she doesn't grow any?"

"No, my lady. She had it planted here in the center, where the mint is. She said it was a form of mint, but not one she wanted to have in what she called her 'life-affirming' maze."

"Did she buy it?" Cecilia pressed.

"No, but she had in the past, I know. Fact is, she and Dr. Patterson agreed it was the right thing to do for Mrs. Morton when she found herself with child after her husband died and her left with five babes, as it were. After the fifth, she was told not to have any more or it would kill her, but that husband of hers thought it all a great hum and insisted on his husbandly rights without doing anything to prevent her quickening with another child. And I know what you're trying to discover, whether my wife provided Miss Inglewood with pennyroyal to shed her unwanted child."

"Lady Aldrich said she overheard Miss Inglewood asking your wife for pennyroyal and Miss Inglewood became irate when she said she wouldn't give her any."

The Vicar let out a large, deep sigh. "Yes. Unfortunately, Miss Inglewood was a bit of a wild child. And the Inglewoods spoiled that girl to imagine the sun rose and set for her. After the girl died, the magistrate came to blame my Miranda for giving her a lethal dose of pennyroyal."

Cecilia frowned. "Yet I heard they say she died of iliac passion."

The vicar spread his hands wide but did not respond. His face looked suddenly pinched, tears began leaking out his eyes and running down his careworn cheeks.

James handed him his handkerchief. The vicar nodded his thanks and blotted his eyes and cheeks. "He visited me last night, you know."

"Who?" Cecilia asked.

"The magistrate. He wants to declare my Miranda committed suicide." He looked from Cecilia to James. "She would never do that."

"Why do you say that?" James asked.

"If she killed herself, she can't be buried here, near me, in our church yard." He wandered out of the garden toward the cemetery. Cecilia and James followed him.

"It would shrivel her soul not to be buried without my giving her God's blessing," he said softly when he stopped for a moment at the gated edge of the church cemetery.

Cecilia shook her head. "I don't understand. Why would he want her to be buried unshriven?"

"I don't know precisely why," he said as he walked on. "All I have are guesses and conjecture. I don't believe Miss Inglewood died from whatever that condition they said is. I believe she died trying to get rid of the babe she carried."

"You think someone else gave her the pennyroyal she had asked your wife for?"

The vicar shrugged, then nodded. "Pennyroyal, tansy, or some other herb that forces the end to an unborn babe."

The vicar stopped on the path that ran through the cemetery toward the almshouses and on to some of the small crofters outside the village. "See that tree there?" he said, pointing to an elm tree off to the side in the cemetery. "I'm going to lay her there unless Squire Inglewood has his way."

"He won't," said James. "There are enough of us who can attest to her position, which was not indicative of how a suicide lands." He reached into a vest pocket and pulled out the brooch. "Is this your wife's brooch?"

The vicar took the brooch from James. "Yes! She wore it nearly every day. How did you come by it?"

"It was found on the other side of the meadow from the escarpment."

"Thank you." He folded his hands over it.

"I'll have to keep it until after the inquisition, as it needs to be presented as evidence."

"Oh… Of course, of course." He handed it back to James.

"I've been told it represents your daughters, Faith and Hope."

He smiled gently, then sank down on a bench at the edge of the cemetery, pulling Cecilia to sit down next to him. "It does," he said heavily. "They were the pride of Miranda's life.

Such beautiful and smart girls." He looked off into the distance, as if he could see them before him.

"Where are they now? They should be informed of their mother's death."

"Yes, yes," he said, then frowned and looked as if he would cry again.

"I don't know where they are or how to reach them," he said brokenly. He lowered his face into his hands.

Wide-eyed at his raw emotional confession, Cecilia reached out a hand to lay on his arm to soothe him.

"Perhaps Mrs. Jones had their direction written down in one journal or another?"

He shook his head without raising his face from his hands.

"Do you know anyone who might know? Anyone who might know how to find them?" James asked.

He lifted his head and thought for a moment. "The earl perhaps. He was instrumental in aiding them in finding positions. They were so angry with Miranda and me when they discovered I was not their natural father." He looked up at them, silently pleading with them to understand. "I knew Miranda was already with child when we wed, but I loved her anyway. I didn't blame her. I knew how convincing some men could be and what false promises they might make."

"You don't have to explain to us. It is obvious you loved your wife in the way you speak of her."

"It was bad of me, but I was glad, for it gave her a reason to marry me. But I held off. You see, I'd loved her for a long while, but a vicar in my circumstances condemns a woman to a life near poverty, in addition to the heaped-on responsibilities in caring for others that not all women want or are capable of carrying. I didn't want that for Miranda.

"But God smiled down on me before Miranda's parents could send her away to have the baby in anonymity and give it up for adoption. I'd completed my training and was serving as a substitute curate while awaiting my assignment. To my surprise, I was offered the position here in Mertonhaugh, a much better position than I feared I might get, as I had no connections as many other young curates had. I hurried to ask her to marry me."

They were all silent for a moment. Cecilia saw an old, stooped woman leave one of the almshouses built of Kentish ragstone and walk in their direction. She wore a drab green dress with a dark-blue shawl wrapped around her. She carried a willow basket and walked slowly with a cane.

"Now is the time to move on to other conversations," Cecilia advised. "After all, this will most likely be brought up again at the inquest this afternoon."

James raised an eyebrow at Cecilia's sudden change of topic but followed her lead. "Vicar, in my temporary role of churchwarden, you were going to show me some of the repairs needed in the church. Perhaps we should discuss those now."

The vicar looked up. "I think that is an admirable idea," he gratefully told James and rose to his feet.

"Cecilia?" asked James

"I will sit here for a while. You go on. I'll catch up later."

Cecilia looked after them as they walked away, and then across the churchyard, not yet turning to recognize the woman who approached. It wasn't until the woman was nearly beside her that Cecilia looked up.

"Hello," she said.

The old woman nodded and, without asking, slowly eased

her body down to sit on the stone bench next to Cecilia. Everything she wore looked old and oft mended, including the mob cap that almost covered her gray, grizzled hair. But her clothing and herself were clean and neat despite her obvious poverty.

She set a rough willow basket on the ground, then placed both hands across each other on the handle of her old cane. Her chin slowly sank to settle on top of her hands.

It looked so like a practiced routine that Cecilia was hard-pressed not to laugh.

"There now," the woman said. "I'd hoped to catch the vicar before he went off again, but the day be yet young. I am Mrs. Hull," she said in a forthright manner, though her voice crackled and hissed with age. There was a lively energy in the woman's eyes that belied her feebleness.

"I am Lady Branstoke," Cecilia returned.

The old woman nodded. Thought for a minute, then continued. "I live down the path here in the last tiny almshouse cottage…at least for now. The vicar wants me to move to the middle one so he might have the end one for the curate he hopes to get, you see." She compressed her lips and shook her head. "But I don't want to move. I like my little house. 'Tisn't much, and I have it fixed up the way I like it. Yes, just the way I like it," she told Cecilia in a manner that sounded quite pleased with herself.

"You are truly fortunate," Cecilia said pleasantly, hoping for an opening to question this woman about Mrs. Jones.

"Could you tell him that?"

"I'm sorry, tell him what?" Cecilia asked.

"That I don't want to move to the middle almshouse," the old woman said matter-of-factly.

"Me?"

"Yes," the woman said, lifting her head from her hands that rested on the cane. "You're a toff. He listens to toffs.—Not that he doesn't listen to others as well, mind you, but he listens to toffs better…" Her brow furrowed. "I suppose we all do if we know what is good fer us."

"I'm sure you can talk him round to your way of thinking," Cecilia said with a smile. "Can I ask you a question?"

"Naturally, you being a lady and all."

The woman's manner amused Cecilia, and she found she quite liked her. She might make a good ally in their investigation. "How well did you know Mrs. Jones?"

"Purty well, if I do say so meself. She helped get me to living in the almshouse when we found out me pension was gone, taken back by my last employer when he lost everything at cards."

"Took your pension? I didn't think that was possible," Cecilia said.

The woman shrugged philosophically. "Don't know how he done it—weren't much—but he done it. But Mrs. Jones, she helped me, she wrote to the Earl of Mortlake on my behalf."

Cecilia's brow furrowed. "Why did she need to appeal to the earl?"

"'Cause he paid for the almshouses here. The old earl did afore him as he built 'em, and now who's ever the current earl gets to say as to who gets to live in 'em."

"I didn't know that!" Cecilia said. "Is the church and all its property in his living?"

"Yes, on account of this used to be the Mortlake family seat when the title came down to him after helping defeat the Roundheads."

"What do you mean when you say: *used to be the family seat?*" Cecilia asked.

"The old earl, he got a bigger, fancy property in Sussex and built a grand house there. Leastwise, that's what they say. They hardly ever visited Mertonhaugh."

"But now they live here," Cecilia stated.

"On account of the fire destroying that grand house. Served him right for abandoning Mertonhaugh, I say."

"You seem to know a great deal about the area."

"Born and bred here, only moved to Maidstone for the years I were in service… Mrs. Jones used to ask me questions about the area all the time, particularly about the people, or I should say the parents and grandparents of the people who are here now. Folks seem to like to talk about their families, and Mrs. Jones told me what I told her gave her the openings she needed to start good conversations."

"Most clever. Do you believe she could have committed suicide?" Cecilia asked.

Mrs. Hull gave a short, soft laugh. "Mrs. Jones? 'Cor, no. She was one to solve problems, not run away from them, if you know what I mean."

"I do, indeed. Did you know her daughters?"

"Faith and Hope? Aye, right nice and proper little gels until they got sent to that fancy school." She shook her head. "Two spoiled gels came home! Not that that were the vicar's and Mrs. Jones' fault. Mrs. Jones confessed to me that their real father wanted them raised a certain way, and not in a way that is correct for people in our positions." She sighed. "They thought themselves above us in the village."

"Oh! You know they are not the vicar's daughters?"

"Aye, but the truth wasn't well known, you know. I guess

Mrs. Jones had'a talk to someone about it, and her someone was me," she said with a little laugh.

"She trusted your discretion," Cecilia said.

Mrs. Hull nodded. "I was blessed," she said. "And I'm the only one she told that Miss Faith sent her a letter two months ago. Said that she knew she and Hope were a mite hasty, and she was sorry for that. She wanted to tell her she was fine and had secured a good position, but didn't tell her where, only that the earl knew."

Cecilia sighed. "Well, that is something, I guess." She stood up. "Let's find the vicar and my husband. I need to return home for a bit before the inquest."

Mrs. Hull rose slowly to her feet. "You watch out for the magistrate at the inquest. He don't like women, or what he thinks of as womanish ways."

"What do you mean?" Cecilia asked as they walked toward the church.

"Won't let his wife and daughter have tea in the afternoon, says that's too womanish and barbaric."

"Womanish?" Cecilia repeated, astonished.

"Yes. That is what he says. Mrs. Hester, she loves the tradition and loves tea. She brings tea down to my little cottage two to three times a week so she might enjoy it. I love the company and the gossip," she said on a coy laugh. "And she leaves what extra tea she has brought with me, so I might enjoy another day of tea."

"That sounds wonderful!" Cecilia said.

Mrs. Hull nodded. "And I *do* need to talk to the vicar. He'll be needing a cook and someone to keep for him; I'd like the job."

Cecilia and Mrs. Hull found the men in the north transept. They were discussing the raised stage the pulpit sat on.

"That floor looks dangerous, Mr. Jones. We need to put this repair at the head of our list lest the wood collapse under you and you fall through the floor."

"I'm sure the lanterns must be more important," Mr. Jones said. "If the floor gave way, you are only talking about a drop of two feet at most."

"But it could be a drop to cause injury, as it would come upon you unawares. It won't take much to put in new floorboards. I'll have the Summerworth carpenter here to fix it before Sunday services. Shouldn't take long."

Mr. Jones looked at the cracking and sagging floorboards and reluctantly agreed. "But lanterns working are important for the congregation."

"Yes, and they will get fixed. Don't you feel it would be nice to have something on your list done? Then you can look forward to getting it all done and not thinking of it as a list that goes nowhere?" James asked.

"James," Cecilia said. "Are you about done here? Hugh needs to be fed before the inquest."

He nodded. "I think we are done here for now anyway," he said.

"And you need to eat, too, Mr. Jones," said Mrs. Hull.

"I'm not hungry, Mrs. Hull."

"Nonsense. You may not feel hungry, but for you to make it through the inquest this afternoon, you'd best have food. I'll nip up to the house and get something for you. Gracious knows I know where everything is. And I can go on cooking and keeping for you, too," she said.

The vicar frowned and shook his head. "I can't think right now, Mrs. Hull."

"I understands, truly," she said soothingly. "I'll just do for you today so you ken see to what ya needs to do, and then we's can talk more on a more permanent situation. Wanted to let you know before that Mrs. Ralston come about offering the same." She shook her head. "Her house ain't tidy like mine.

"I ain't braggin', but I wanna help today. Also, wanna let you know I's interested afore Mrs. Ralston come offering the same. Asides, I cain't abide havin' nothin' to do. That's why I helped with Miranda's garden and do trimming around some of the headstones."

The vicar looked bemused and a bit hunted.

Cecilia and James tried to hide their laughter at the competition forming between the neighbor ladies, and Mrs. Jones was not even in the grave yet.

The Branstokes took their leave of the vicar, saying they would see him at the inquest that afternoon. In the meantime, they were going to see the earl to see if he knew where to find Hope and Faith. They wanted to send express messages to both young women.

CHAPTER 5

The inquest was to be held in the basement of the Mortlake Brewery. They went in through an outside basement entry on the east side of the brewery, where casks and barrels of beer and ale were taken out of the building for loading into wagons for delivery. Halfway down the wide stone steps, Cecilia smelled the damp walls and felt the cold basement air, first around her ankles, then further up her body as she continued down. She drew her shawl closer around her shoulders. Ahead was a wide corridor lined on either side with brewery barrels and other barrels, including a large tun at the end and other, smaller-sized casks.

The walls were brick-covered, with a lime-wash that appeared creamy yellow in the light of the overhead gas lanterns held near the ceiling by chains on pulleys tied off by iron cleats mounted on the wall.

She and James followed those before them down the corridor to a room off to the right. The arched opening led to a square room. Placed in the middle of the room was a six-foot-long trestle table covered with a white cloth on which the body of Mrs. Jones had been placed, covered with another white cloth. Cecilia unconsciously raised her hand to her heart on seeing Mrs. Jones' shrouded form. She told herself before they came that she could not cry. That admonition to herself might be harder to adhere to than she thought.

Before them in the room, standing at the head of the table, were the magistrate, the coroner—who Cecilia knew to be Mr. Wilfred Davos—the coroner's clerk, and Dr. Patterson.

Other people were crowding into the room, sorting themselves out into the jurors, the witnesses, and the curious. Cecilia, along with James and Lord Aldrich, found themselves standing near the head of the table by Dr. Patterson. The curious stood close together at the back of the room and included the Earl of Mortlake and his son, Viscount Kendell. Looking about, Cecilia observed that she was the only woman present.

"I call this inquest to order," said the coroner, Mr. Wilfred Davos. "Mr. Woodbine, please read the summation."

"Yes, sir, Mr. Davos," Mr. Woodbine said, his clogged, reedy voice clearing, then continuing. "This is the inquest into the death of Mrs. Miranda Jones, wife of Vicar Mr. Septimus Jones. A resident of Mertonhaugh for twenty-two years."

"Magistrate Squire Inglewood, if you would start with how you came to know about this death and a description of the scene when you arrived," declared Mr. Davos.

"Lord Aldrich came to me to report that Mrs. Jones' body was seen at the base of a cliff off the Haughton Meadow. His arrival nearly coincided with Vicar Jones coming to relate that his wife did not come home last night, and not an hour previously, her horse had turned up riderless at the Mortlake stables. I notified Dr. Patterson and invited him to accompany us to collect the body. Lord Aldrich contacted Mr. Haydon Veron for the use of his wagon. I requested the vicar stay behind."

"Why did you do that?" the coroner asked.

Precisely my question! Cecilia said to herself. *Such a lack of feeling.*

"I did not want any emotionality at the site of a suspicious death. It can cloud an investigation," he answered crisply.

Cecilia raised her eyebrows and slid a glance at her husband. He had his arms crossed over his chest and frowned.

"To continue, if I might, at the meadow, I discovered Lady Branstoke and Lady Aldrich with their young children. They had been on the meadow for a picnic. Sir James Branstoke had climbed down the escarpment to examine the body and was climbing back up when we arrived at the scene."

Cecilia watched him rock back on his heels and draw himself up as he drew a breath to continue his testimony. He was planning something, she was sure of it.

"Mrs. Jones lay some forty to fifty feet down the escarpment on Haughton Meadow off the road that leads from Mertonhaugh to the dry valley," he continued. "From where I stood at the top of the cliff, it was clear she was deceased. When the others brought her up, there were no signs of any marks on her body other than what she'd received from falling."

"To be clear," interrupted the coroner again, "you did not participate in retrieving Mrs. Jones from where she'd fallen?"

The magistrate raised his chin. "No. I deemed it more important to look around for any other signs of someone being in the area."

"And did you find any?" the coroner continued.

"No."

"But surely you would have at least seen evidence of the Branstokes and the Aldriches being in the meadow?"

"Well, yes, of course," Inglewood said irritably.

"How did you conclude no one else had been on the meadow?"

"I looked for trampled grass and saw none. It is my considered conclusion that the woman committed suicide because of her culpability in the death of my daughter, Georgia Inglewood."

The room exploded with an equal measure of agreement and protest. Voices shouted above each other to get their viewpoints heard.

"Silence! Silence!" demanded the coroner, pounding on the desk before him. "Silence, I say.

"Squire Inglewood, you are being impertinent and should know that in your position. We are not at any point to declare with any certainty the cause of death. And with regards to your daughter, it was determined to be iliac passion, isn't that correct?" he said strongly.

Cecilia arched her brows, for to her eye, his expression and posture looked heavy with silent communication. She turned her head slightly to glance at her husband. With a slight dip of his chin, he acknowledged he saw something as well.

"Remember?" the coroner continued. "We are all sorry for your daughter's death. Do not turn your daughter's passing into something else. Her cause of death is God-given, not person-given. *As you agreed*," he finished tightly.

Squire Inglewood's jaw tightened, and he glared back at

the coroner. Then he saw others staring at him. He turned his head and licked his lips as he relaxed his features.

Dr. Patterson, his arms crossed over his chest, scowled.

"We shall continue with witness testimony," Mr. Davos said.

The clerk cleared his throat. "Dr. Patterson."

The coroner nodded. "Dr. Patterson, please tell us the state of the deceased when you examined her."

"I rappelled down the cliff side after Mr. Vernon. Mrs. Jones was lying almost on her back side, her head pointing down the cliff. It was evident she had only recently died, as her skin was still warm and rigor mortis had not set in. There were no signs of a struggle on her body, no scratches or disheveled clothing, no bruises that could not be accounted for by an attack upon her person. I believe she fell backward off the cliff. Whether she was pushed or fell, I cannot judge.

"She broke her right hip and leg, crushed her right shoulder, broke a couple of ribs, broke her left ankle, and took a severe blow to her head from a rock her head landed on." He turned her head so the jurors could see the wound on the side of her head. He pointed to the area.

"She bled from this spot, and there was an associated puddle of blood on the rock her head lay against. Chalk and dirt particles were in the wound, indicating a fall against the ground, not a blow to the head. She wore a glove on her left hand, but not on her right. The fingernails of her right hand were clean and even.

"Given her age and the extent of her injuries, I do not think she could have recovered even if someone had gone for help immediately."

Dr. Patterson looked across at the jurors. "Upon complete

examination of the body after she was brought here, I have no additional observations."

The coroner nodded. "I concur."

Mr. Woodbine sanded what he'd written, then stood up to call the next witness. "Sir James Branstoke."

"Sir James, had you ever been on that meadow before?" asked the coroner.

"I've ridden across one side of it to take the road to the valley on the other side; however, I've never spent any time on the meadow, no."

"How long have you lived in the area?" asked the coroner.

"Two years. Since I purchased the Summerworth property from the Duke of Monteith."

The coroner nodded and waited a moment for his clerk to finish recording the last statements. "Sir James, if you would, please, describe how you discovered the deceased."

"I was lying on the picnic blanket next to my young son when I realized he needed his mother's attention. I picked him up and carried him across the meadow to where my wife was standing, guarding the approach to the escarpment from Miss Charlotte Aldrich, who had been running around the meadow."

"Miss Charlotte Aldrich?" repeated Mr. Woodbine, brow furrowed.

"My one-year-old daughter," Lord Aldrich explained.

"So not another witness," stated Mr. Woodbine as he made further notes.

"No," Lord Aldrich said while others in the room laughed.

James smiled and continued. "After I passed my malodorous heir to my wife, I stepped back to look down the escarpment."

"Why?" asked the magistrate.

The coroner scowled at the magistrate.

Sir James shrugged. "Curiosity. I'd not spent time on that meadow before and wanted to see how steep the escarpment was. That is when I saw the body about forty feet down, as the magistrate described."

"What did you do when you saw her?"

"I called Lord Aldrich to come see. At that time, we didn't immediately know who the woman was. It was Lady Branstoke who identified the deceased as Mrs. Jones."

"Between Aldrich and me, we decided he would ride back to the village to notify the magistrate and collect people to fetch Mrs. Jones from her position on the cliff. While he did that, our wives would pack the picnic things away and attend to the children."

"There were no servants with you, Sir James?" asked the coroner.

"No, it was an informal picnic. No need to take the staff away from their duties," James said.

There was a murmur of voices among others in the room that the coroner hushed with a glare.

"What did you do while Lord Aldrich was gone?"

"I decided to find a way to climb down the cliff face to get to Mrs. Jones, to verify she was deceased, and perhaps be able to judge how long she'd been deceased by touching her."

"You would have the knowledge to do that?" asked the coroner incredulously.

"I spent several years with Wellington's army during the Peninsular War. Yes, I can judge the deceased," he said in his typical calm fashion, though his eyes were sharp as he looked back at the coroner.

The coroner coughed. "Yes, I suppose that might grant you that knowledge."

"To continue, I removed my boots and jacket and, at the suggestion of my wife, pulled on my riding gloves to protect my fingers from the sharp rocks. I did not descend directly above Mrs. Jones. The ground there was unstable and showed signs of slippage. About ten to fifteen feet to the side, I saw what looked to be better handholds and toeholds for descending."

"You did not repel like the magistrate did?" asked the coroner.

James shook his head. "We did not have a rope among our picnic supplies.

"I made my way over to her," he continued. "When I was by her side, I touched the side of her neck. I was surprised to feel a light, fluttering pulse."

"But she was dead by the time I touched her," Dr. Patterson interjected.

James relaxed. "By then, yes. May I continue?"

"Yes, Sir James, please do," said the coroner, his clerk beside him writing furiously.

"I spoke to her, and she reached out to grab my shirtsleeve. Her grip was surprisingly strong. She asked for water. My wife lowered down to us water I could pour onto her lips and into her mouth."

"I thought you said you didn't have a rope," the magistrate protested.

"We didn't. Lady Branstoke took one of the cart reins and tied it to the handle of a picnic basket and that way lowered a water pouch to me... After drinking the water, Mrs. Jones tried to speak. She seemed to be gathering whatever strength

remained in her body. She grew agitated. She said... *No...
penny...roy... Stop,*" he said carefully.

"No pennyroy stop?" repeated the clerk. "What does that
mean?"

"The last thing she said to her killer?" Sir James suggested.
"Telling whoever was there with her that she did not have any
pennyroyal. I don't know; however, simply saying those few
words sapped the last of her strength. She slipped into unconsciousness. I stayed with her, afraid she was near the end, and
I didn't want her to die alone. It was about twenty minutes
later that the death rattles began with its terrible breathing."

The crowd murmured among themselves at the end of his
testimony.

"Thank you, Sir James," said the coroner. He looked at his
clerk. "Next?"

"Lady Branstoke," read the clerk from his list.

"We don't need Lady Branstoke's testimony," protested the
magistrate. "Her husband can speak for her."

"I assure you, we do." Sir James said.

"She has an uncanny way of observing things others miss,"
replied the coroner. "We should hear her testimony."

The magistrate folded his arms across his chest. "Waste of
time," he muttered, glaring at the Branstokes.

"Lady Branstoke," began the coroner, "you are the wife of
Sir James Branstoke."

She answered affirmatively.

"And you have resided in Mertonhaugh for the past two
years... Please tell us your observations."

"I saw Mrs. Jones lying nearly on her back, as Dr.
Patterson described. Besides the blood from her head, blood
had also seeped from her mouth. Her right arm was bent at an

odd angle, but her left arm lay across her body, her hand open, palm down, and lay across her heart. Her fingers were where she'd typically pinned her cameo brooch. Her eyes were closed—which I surmised meant she'd had an opportunity to close her eyes after her fall, as it also looked like she had been able to move her left arm."

"Why do you believe she had moved?" the coroner asked.

"I say that because there was white chalk visible on her sleeve." Cecilia demonstrated on her own arm where the white chalk had shown on Mrs. Jones, and how the white chalk must have gotten on the sleeve when she first fell, then, when she'd picked her arm up, the white chalk had become visible on the top of her body.

"She'd lost the brooch in the meadow, most likely that same day," she continued.

The coroner pounced. "How can you say that?"

"Because Miss Charlotte Aldrich found the brooch in the grass at the other side of the meadow from the escarpment. Lady Aldrich and I recognized the jewelry as belonging to Mrs. Jones."

"Where is that brooch now?" asked the coroner. "We can ask Mr. Jones to verify the item."

"It's right here," Cecilia said as she pulled it out of her reticule.

Mr. Jones could not help giving a little inarticulate cry at seeing it again. Cecilia handed it to him. Tears streamed down his face. "Yes, yes," he choked out. "This is Miranda's. For her, it represented our daughters, Faith and Hope, who left the village three years ago."

"Mr. Davos, might I continue?" Cecilia asked after the room quieted.

He nodded. "Yes, proceed."

"I did not see any evidence of a conveyance or horse in the area, nor signs of one, though I did look about. That could mean she walked up to the meadow; however, I don't feel that likely. Vicar, could she have done that?"

"No, the arthritis in her knees meant she rode in her cart most everywhere. Or, she rode up to the meadow."

The Earl of Mortlake raised his hand, and the coroner acknowledged him.

"The horse Mrs. Jones rides arrived last night at the Mortlake stables—still saddled. I gave her the horse last March."

"You gave her the horse?"

"Yes, it was Lady Mortlake's saddle horse that had become too old to be ridden in the fashion my wife prefers. I bought her a new mare before the holidays. Rather than having another horse to keep, I offered the mare to the Vicar and his wife."

Cecilia raised her hand.

"My lady?" acknowledged the coroner.

"Were her painting supplies still on the horse?" she asked the earl.

The earl raised his chin as he nodded slightly at her question, his eyes thoughtful. "I couldn't say to that, Lady Branstoke. Nothing was said of what was with the saddle. I should have to ask my grooms."

She nodded, her lips compressing as she considered the implications of the presence, or absence, of painting supplies.

"Thank you, my lord," said the coroner with a bow of his head.

Next, Lord Aldrich and Mr. Vernon were interviewed. They had nothing more to add to what Branstoke said. Cecilia's thoughts wandered as they spoke, and she stared down at the still body of what once had been an active, smiling woman.

She had to have been with someone, Cecilia thought. Even if she simply fell backward, why wouldn't whoever she was with go to get help? Had someone wanted her to die, whether they were the active agent of her death or not? She couldn't imagine that poor woman lying there, helpless for so long, perhaps crying out for help, but left there to die.

When no more witnesses came forward, the coroner asked the jury for a conclusion. The jury went into another room in the basement for their discussion, but soon returned.

"Jury, you have heard the testimony from the witnesses. What is your conclusion?" the coroner asked. "Accidental death or death by person or persons unknown?"

The jurors agreed, manslaughter by person or persons unknown.

"Manslaughter?" queried the magistrate, obviously irate at their conclusion.

"Aye, sir. Two of us knows that cliff well. If it be in the condition described by Lord and Lady Branstoke, it likely crumbled underfoot, causing Mrs. Jones to fall backward. Howsomever, she knew that cliff. She would nary 'ave gone close to it if'n someone hadn't cornered her or chased her there, and with her jewelry on the other side of the meadow, stands to reason she were not alone," said Mr. Altman.

"What about suicide?" the magistrate pressed.

Mr. Altman scratched his head. "I don't see as how someone would go backward and land on their back if'n it were suicide. Don't make no sense, physical-like, and not make a bit o' sense to us who knowed her."

The magistrate chuffed.

The coroner thanked the jury for their service, and the inquest was adjourned.

As she and James followed the crowd of people who had attended the inquest back up the stairs and into daylight, Cecilia felt satisfied with the verdict. Particularly satisfied that the magistrate did not get his suicide verdict!

But there was still the matter of who had been on the meadow with Mrs. Jones and what had been their intent? Why were they with Mrs. Jones?

"Sir James! Lady Branstoke!" hailed the Earl of Mortlake. He waved his son to proceed on without him while he waited for them.

"I want to thank you for your testimony on behalf of Mrs. Jones—and you, Sir James, for your care of her." His face drew together in a scowl. "I am quite put out with the bumptious behavior of our magistrate. I sense his position has damaged him. Pity. I used to like the fellow. We were at university together for a short time."

Cecilia couldn't help but smile at his last statement.

"It was the least I could do for the woman," James said. "She was more than the vicar's wife. She was an asset to our village."

"I concur —I'd like you and Lady Branstoke to join my wife and me for dinner tonight. I know it is a last-minute invitation; however, I have a request for both of you that you are eminently suited to fulfill."

Cecilia and Sir James exchanged glances. Cecilia raised an eyebrow at her husband to indicate that it was his decision.

Sir James looked back at the earl. "We shall be delighted to join you this evening."

After exchanging details, the Branstokes parted from Mortlake and returned to Summerworth Park.

CHAPTER 6

THE EARL'S CONFESSION

"James, why has Mortlake invited us to dinner tonight?" Cecilia asked when he'd wandered into her dressing room, attired for the evening.

"I don't know," James said as he adjusted the cuffs of his shirt under his jacket. "But it falls in line with our needs, so I am more than happy to have dinner with them."

"Yes, I know," said Cecilia. Seated at her dressing table, she looked into her mirror at her lady's maid. "Sarah, stop fussing. It looks suitable for dinner at a neighbor's. We are not going to a ball!" she admonished Sarah with a gentle smile.

Sarah ruefully backed away. Cecilia rose and turned toward James. "I would like to understand his motivations. Does he want something from us? I don't expect this to be a casual dinner event."

James looked at Cecilia. "No, you're probably correct. However, it doesn't do us any good to ponder the whys and the wherefores at this time. If you are ready, we should make our way downstairs. I ordered the coach to go to the Mortlake estate."

"Not your phaeton?" Cecilia asked.

"No," James said with a slight smile.

Cecilia looked at him and smiled back, knowing they would have George Romley as their coachman. Romley would question the grooms about Mrs. Jones's horse, among other things.

She and James were often of a like mind on their inquiries without a word spoken between them. "Yes, of course," she said instead. "Let me grab my shawl." She picked up her beautiful Indian silk shawl, which her lady's maid had laid out for her. It had been a gift from Rani, sent from India. She followed James out of her dressing room.

He took her arm in his as they walked down the stairs and out of the door to their coach.

THE TRIP to the Mortlake estate was quick. They did not live far from them, though the Mortlake estate properties extended quite a way in the other direction. They were almost their closest neighbor, aside from the Aldriches.

When they arrived at the estate, the Mortlake butler was awaiting them and quickly escorted them inside. Mortlake came out of the drawing room to the right. The earl was a tall man, nearly as tall as Sir James, and walked with an extremely upright posture. Eschewing the somber gray he'd worn at the inquest, he'd donned a bottle-green jacket over a muted green and brown striped waistcoat. He wore his curly, liberally gray-streaked brown hair brushed back away from his prominent forehead and cut to his collar in the back.

"Welcome, welcome. I'm glad you could come. Come on in

here. Dinner will be served shortly, but can I get you a preprandial?"

They agreed to a drink and followed the earl into a beautifully accoutered pale-green drawing room done in the Georgian style with white panel moldings and tasteful peach-colored accents. Lady Mortlake sat on a peach sofa, acknowledging their entry with a smile, a softly spoken *hello*, and a gracious incline of her head. Though a blonde fading to gray, she was still a striking woman with few lines on her face. Her bronze gown of the latest fashion shimmered in the candlelight.

With a wave of his hand, the earl indicated Cecilia should join his wife on the sofa and Sir James the chair to the left while he poured their drinks. As smiling and gracious as Lady Mortlake's manner was, to Cecilia's eye, she seemed stiff, her features tight. Cecilia felt that the woman wasn't pleased with their being at their home for dinner. But as this was an invitation her husband had extended, she appeared determined to play the gracious hostess.

The earl handed Cecilia a glass of sherry and one to his wife as well, then handed James a glass of port. Then he sat down in the chair at a right angle to where his wife sat on the sofa, and easily crossed his long legs.

He held his glass loosely between his fingers as he soberly looked at them. "I'm sure you're curious as to why I invited you here for dinner." He straightened slightly. "We have been meaning to do so for a while, but with your having a young son, we haven't done so. However, with the events that occurred yesterday, I felt it behooved us to get better acquainted."

"Agreed," James said before he took a sip of port.

"We have heard of your investigative exploits," Mortlake continued. "Deaths, thefts, kidnappings, and wrongful arrests..." He shook his head. "Your amazing reputation precedes you."

Cecilia laughed and demurred. "I wouldn't say amazing. Curious, perhaps, but not intentional."

Sir James smiled at his wife as he nodded.

The earl waved his hand negligently. "Regardless of whether intentional or not, I should like to request your services to carefully investigate the situation surrounding Mrs. Jones's death."

James and Cecilia exchanged glances. "No need to make a request," Sir James said smoothly as he relaxed back into his chair. "We have already determined to do so."

The earl nodded. "Good. I think..." he said slowly, first looking toward his wife before he continued, "I need to provide you a bit more information regarding Mrs. Jones. She probably has more friends than enemies; however, those enemies could be more dangerous than others."

"Dangerous?" Sir James echoed, a dark brow rising.

Mortlake uncrossed his legs, sat straighter, and took a large drink of his port before he continued. "As you might have heard by now, the Joneses have two daughters, Faith and Hope. They are twins in their early twenties—two years older than my son, the viscount."

"Yes, the vicar told us."

The earl nodded. He set his glass on the table placed beside his chair and rested his elbows on the chair arms, steepling his fingers. He took a deep breath and blew it out. "They are actually my daughters," he confessed.

Sir James and Cecilia looked at each other, but did not interrupt.

"Miranda and I had an affair when I was still at the university. And being young, impetuous, and stupid, I took advantage of a very nice and decent young woman."

Cecilia looked over at Lady Mortlake. She sat studiously looking down at her hands, clasping her glass. Cecilia looked back at the Earl of Mortlake.

"Of course, my father did not want me to have to marry Miranda; she did not come from a family considered worthy of the Countess title, and I can't say I desired marriage with her. I was a young and foolish man—without proper regard for a gently reared woman—feeling his oats. But Father said we must make what amends as we could and help her and the unborn babe as much as possible. At that time, we thought it was only one child.

"Father sent Mr. Bennett, one of his estate stewards, to investigate Miranda and to see if there were any young men in the area who might want to marry her. From gossip in the village tavern, he learned Septimus Jones was sweet on her. Some tavern patrons teased him about her and how she was looking higher than a curate. Mr. Jones was growing angry at how they were bantering her name around, so Mr. Bennett got him out of there before any fights broke out."

He stopped for a moment to take a sip of his drink. "It was a fortuitous meeting," he continued. "They talked, and Jones admitted he loved Miranda and had for years, but was afraid to approach her because, unfortunately, she had stars in her eyes when she looked at me," the earl admitted, wincing.

"Father did some investigation and discovered that

Septimus Jones was looking for a position. He did not have the connections many others did, being younger sons of aristocracy, when they completed seminary training. As it happened, the Mortlake living here in Mertonhaugh was in need of a new vicar. Not many people realized it was part of the Mortlake estate, as this is not our principal property. My grandfather built a new, larger estate in Sussex that we adopted as the Mortlake seat.

"Father arranged for Mr. Jones to be offered the living in Mertonhaugh. Jones was naturally surprised when he was offered the living and, for a time, did not know it was connected to my family. Mr. Bennett congratulated him and said he now would have the funds to support a wife, and he encouraged him to ask Miranda to marry him.

"By that time, Mr. Jones knew she was with child but said he still wanted to marry her. Miranda was despondent, but at the same time grateful, and she went ahead and married Septimus Jones. After the wedding they came here, to Mertonhaugh.

"I did not come here. I stayed at our other estate in Sussex. I did not feel that I should put myself forward in any way that would cause her or Mr. Jones discomfort. We—particularly my father—wanted the best for them. He never held her at fault."

"Your father sounds like he was a very good man," James said.

Mortlake smiled. "Yes, he was. He was strict in many ways, but he was a good man. Then I met Clementia, here," he said, looking at his wife, "and fell in love with her."

Cecilia saw Lady Mortlake look up at him then, and they

exchanged smiles. She was gratified to see that the story the earl was telling them had not harmed their relationship.

Mortlake looked back at Sir James and Cecilia. "Father insisted that I tell her everything, that there should be no secrets in our marriage, and I have." He looked again at his wife and this time reached out his hand to hers and squeezed it. "It was she who encouraged me to see that the girls had good educations and did not lack for the things young girls love."

He dropped her hand and continued more soberly. "We have had a good marriage. I'm incredibly happy. We have only been blessed with one child, but we are happy."

He frowned. "Then there was a fire at our Sussex estate when Lady Mortlake and I were in London. Burned it to the ground. It had been such a hot, fast fire, many died, including my father. I couldn't face rebuilding the manor immediately, so we came here. It was the original property granted by the king in the 1600s. I decided, as the new earl, it was time that I came to honor this property while I decided what to do about Sussex."

Sir James nodded. "And that is when you met your daughters."

"Frankly, that wasn't a consideration. The two girls would have been grown by then, around nineteen years old. As far as I knew, they could have been married or had positions somewhere. So we came here. And I quickly discovered my girls were living here."

Cecilia's attention perked at hearing him call his daughters "my girls."

"They had stayed longer at the finishing school upon graduation to take on teacher positions there for a year. But by the time we came to Mertonhaugh, they'd decided they wanted to go out on their own, so they'd returned home to the Jones as they were searching for positions."

"Would you have come here if you'd known they were here?" Cecilia asked, sliding a glance in Lady Mortlake's direction.

"I'd like to think so. I was delighted to meet them. Both of us were," he said, turning toward his wife.

She nodded.

"They were beautiful young ladies, and in my eagerness to get to know them, I confessed to them that I am their father. They had not known they were not the vicar's natural children, and they did not take the news well. They became angry with their mother for not letting them know the truth."

"Why should she have?" asked Sir James.

"Precisely," declared Lady Mortlake. It was the first thing she'd said since the discussion began. "It was obvious to all that Mr. Jones loved them. He always felt as if they were his own daughters."

"They'd seen evidence at the school of how the girls, who were known to be illegitimate children, were treated," Mortlake continued. "And they were horrified that they fell into that same category. And from what I understand, they might have been guilty of teasing some of those girls in a way that was not Christian," he finished slowly.

"Ah," said Cecilia. "Their own guilt fueled their anger at their mother."

"So we believe," said Lady Mortlake. "They made the rash decision that they were going to find positions far away and never return. Miranda was quite distraught. I told her Mortlake would help them find positions, and that way, we could ensure they were safe. She was relieved."

"And I did," said Mortlake. "Faith is a governess for the Duke of Monteith in Devon."

"Monteith!" Cecilia exclaimed while Sir James laughed.

"By your surprise, am I to assume you know him?" Mortlake asked, looking from one to the other.

Now Cecilia laughed. "I have not yet had the opportunity to meet him; however, it is only a matter of time."

Sir James looked at Mortlake. "Monteith is my cousin. I purchased Summerworth Park from him."

"Ah!" said Mortlake. "He was here at the time, looking over the property and what repairs needed to be done before it was sold. We invited him to dinner, and that is when we learned he was looking for a governess for his daughter, Chelsea."

"I recommended Faith Jones, as I knew she wanted to be a governess," said Lady Mortlake.

Cecilia nodded. "Well done."

"Forgive my curiosity, how did you come to own Summerworth?" the earl asked Sir James.

"He wrote me telling me of his plans to sell Summerworth. I asked him to sell it to me before he tried to sell it out of the family. I could also give him a better price, and I did not need to have repairs made. That would have drained his pocketbook even more."

"What of the other Miss Jones?" Cecilia asked. "Hope, I think?"

"I heard from some friends that Lady Falsworth was seeking a companion," Lady Mortlake said.

"Lady Falsworth?" Sir James said. "I wouldn't have judged her to be of an age to have wanted a companion."

"From my understanding, she liked to travel and didn't want to do so by herself. Hope had one time said to us, quite wistfully, that she would like to travel. It did not take much to pair her with Lady Falsworth," Lady Mortlake said with a quiet laugh. "They've been gone quite a bit, not into Europe, but traveling around Scotland and England, for Lady Falsworth is quite a history fanatic, particularly about anything from the Roman invasion."

"Lady Falsworth intends to write a book of her travels and observations. My daughter has also become her amanuensis," said Mortlake.

"It sounds like you have paid attention to the activities of your daughters," Sir James observed.

"Yes, I have. As we assisted them in securing positions, I wanted to make sure that they would at least have good lives. I would be happier if they could each meet some young man and marry. However, that is not for me to guide them. They must make their own way," said Mortlake.

His wife nodded. "Unfortunately, as all this became known, many people lost respect for Mrs. Jones, which quite distressed me. She was a woman worthy of respect. I quite liked her. She treated everybody well. She tended the ill and the indigent, making care packages and medicines and the like. She was quite dutiful in her rounds as a vicar's wife. Like she was made for that role!"

"I always thought so," said Cecilia.

"As she was also a talented herbalist, it is said Georgia Inglewood went to her to get rid of the baby she carried. I don't know if anybody knew who the father was, but evidently, it was somebody that the Inglewoods would not have been happy to accept as their son-in-law. Mrs. Jones refused."

"So we have heard."

"They had quite a row. It was heard by several in the village. It is said that Miss Inglewood was heard throwing crockery at Mrs. Jones. Three days later, when Georgia died, it was the gossips that said Mrs. Jones played a role in her death."

"Gossip is the lifeblood of Mertonhaugh," drawled Cecilia darkly.

"Didn't they declare her death to be due to iliac passion?" Sir James asked.

Lord Mortlake nodded. "Yes, that is what they recorded. However, it was a closed inquest. Not many people were there, and particularly, the doctor was not there. It has been rumored since that Miss Inglewood might have actually committed suicide."

"Well," Lady Mortlake fairly tittered, "that was something that Inglewood would not want to get out at all, because that would mean his daughter would be buried unshriven and not be in the church's consecrated graveyard."

It is obvious that Lady Mortlake does not like Squire Inglewood, Cecilia mused.

"But more are of the mind that Mrs. Jones relented and gave her a potion to rid her of the baby. An abortifacient that did not work, but instead caused her death," Mortlake added.

"I see," said Cecilia. "Do you feel that Mrs. Jones would have done that?"

"Absolutely not," stated Mortlake. "Clementina, what are your thoughts?"

"No, I do not believe so, either. She was a very good

woman. I'd become quite fond of her in the time since we've been here."

"Father," began Viscount Kendell, pushing open the drawing room doors. "Oh, beg your pardon, I didn't realize you were entertaining," he said, turning to leave.

"Don't go. Please come in and join us," Mortlake called out to his son. "You might be able to assist us. Do you know anyone who might have wanted to kill Mrs. Jones?"

"Probably anyone who thought she'd procured pennyroyal for Miss Inglewood."

"What do you mean?"

"From my understanding, it's an herb women use to get rid of unwanted pregnancies."

"Good gracious, how did you come to know such things to even talk about it?" his mother asked.

He laughed. "I'm not a little boy any longer, Mother; such things are well known in my circle of friends."

"That's disgusting," his mother protested.

"Do not be naïve, Mother. You know Father got Mrs. Jones enceinte when he was at university."

"Yes, but he did not encourage her to rid her body of the babes. I wasn't aware you knew."

Her son laughed. "Father told me a long time ago. And if he hadn't, I would have heard it from many others in town; it isn't exactly a secret, particularly since you and father moved here after the fire to our house in Sussex while I was at university. I've always regretted being away at school and not being able to meet my sisters before they took positions elsewhere. It would have been nice to get to know them after growing up as an only child."

"I agree," said the Earl. "Unfortunately, they were quite

angry to learn that the Vicar was not their father and felt their mother betrayed them by not telling them. They left the area due to that anger and I don't believe they have been reconciled."

"The vicar said he doesn't know how to communicate with them to tell them of their mother's death," Sir James said.

"I do," said the Earl. "I have already undertaken to inform them. Hope is not far away, as Lady Falsworth is currently in London; however, Faith is farther away, in Devon."

"Father, what if I take a letter to Faith? I can get there faster than by post."

"I don't think that is the best way for you to meet," the earl said dryly.

"But—"

"Captain Horsley is in port at Folkestone with the yacht. I contacted him this morning. He might well be away by now, depending on the tides. I am sending him to make a personal delivery. Traveling by water will be quicker than going by horse. He can bring her back the same way, should she wish to come."

"What about Miss Hope Jones?"

"I have sent Jimmy Puller with a letter and our traveling chaise to fetch her, if she chooses to come."

"You keep saying: *if she chooses*," Sir James observed. "Why wouldn't they come at word of their mother's death?"

"They were unhappy that they did not know they were not the vicar's daughters, and I admit I rather crassly announced it when I met them in town. They had had no idea, and I bumbled into that lack of knowledge. They had been looking for positions for some time, but not aggressively. When they learned the truth and the gossips in the village had it on the tips of their tongues, they decided they must leave."

"Why have their locations been secret?"

"It is what they wanted. I don't know why. It has been three years since they left. Hopefully, they will have forgiven their mother in some way."

"I hope so," Cecilia said softly.

"If you don't mind, I should like to change the subject of our conversation to something perhaps less melancholy," Sir James said.

"I welcome it," said Mortlake.

"Tell me about your brewery. I've noted that your brewmaster is young for that position."

"Haydon Vernon?" Mortlake laughed. "Don't let his youth fool you. He has been involved in beer brewing since he could walk! His father was our former brewmaster and well-known among brewers for his talent. Many tried to hire him away from me, but he wouldn't go as his family was from the area. Haydon learned from him, and now he is being courted just as his father was. We have been so successful with Haydon as the brewmaster that I am looking to expand the brewery. I've hired the architect who designed the Raleigh Brewery to do designs for us."

"Your plans might dovetail well with my plans," said Sir James. "I am planning to build an oast house."

Mortlake laughed. "Competition for mine?"

"I'd like to consider mine as complementing yours. I do not want to see a repeat of last year with our cool summer when harvests quickly became musty if they could not be processed quickly."

Mortlake frowned and reluctantly nodded. "That was a

bad time. My apologies if you lost much. And I can see that with my expanded brewery, I shall need more dried barley and hops. I suppose I must welcome your oast house—until I can see my way clear to expanding that facility as well," he said with a side smirk.

"Excuse me, my lord," said the Mortlake butler from the doorway. "Dinner is served."

"Excellent!" Mortlake said. He rose from his seat and motioned the others to follow him to the dining room.

CHAPTER 7

GOSSIP AND CASUAL CONVERSATIONS

The sunlight through the apse windows shone down on the pulpit as Sir James and the Summerworth carpenter, Elmore McCurdy, studied the pulpit platform. In the bright, unexpected sunlight, James could see that the platform was in worse shape than he'd observed the previous day.

"What do you think, Mr. McCurdy? Can this be fixed before Sunday services?"

"Och, aye, sar, if'n I takes off the skirt with the decorative carving nice and easy-like, to build the platform, can be done in a tick. Then we stain it and put back these purty skirt pieces, and it be better than ever. You want as how I should go ahead and do this?"

"What other jobs do you have?"

"Reet now only a new gate in the back pasture."

"The one we talked about connecting to the Aldrich property?"

"That be the one. And the new bed for young Master Hugh."

James nodded. "Both of those can wait on the church

repairs. I'd like this platform completed first, then the Vicar has other repairs here I'd like you to look at as well. Take as long as you like on the repairs for the church property. The vicar needs a good ear right now."

"I catch your meanin', sar. I'd be happy to," the carpenter said, with a wide grin and a conspiratorial wink.

James laughed. "Good man. Let's find the vicar and tell him you are at his disposal to attend to the repairs."

"Reet behind ya, sar," Mr. McCurdy said as James walked out the side door of the church.

They found Mr. Jones at the open door of the rectory, glowering after a visitor who scuttled away.

"Mr. Jones, is there a problem?" James asked.

"What?" Mr. Jones said, jerked out of his thoughts. He turned toward Sir James. "That is the second person in two days to *gently* suggest my Miranda accidentally killed Miss Inglewood with her tisane. Thought that explained my wife's death, that she took her own life in guilt and sorrow, never no mind what the inquest said." The vicar shook his head, then ran his hand through his sparse white hair. "This village likes its drama and will make it up out of whole cloth if they need to. –But I'm sorry, I'm sure you didn't come here to discuss the unfortunate gossip."

"Hardly," agreed James. "I've brought Mr. McCurdy around to survey repairs to be done here. He tells me they will be straightforward."

"Aye," said Mr. McCurdy. "Work be slow up at the Park now. I'd be reet glad to busy ma hands with work. And I wouldna mind but to put a bee in an ear of any who want to come by to speak badly of yur missus. She were a good woman."

The vicar smiled slightly. "Thank you, Mr. McCurdy."

"I'm a goin' to hie meself on up to the Park now to git ma tools, and I'll be back after noonins." He reset his cap on his head, and after a nod to both of them, he trotted down the road toward Summerworth Park.

"I'm hearing noises from inside your house," James observed after Mr. McCurdy left.

"Mrs. Hull. She simply came and started doing for me. I didn't have much say, other than I know of other parties who want to do the housekeeping and cooking for me. Did make a fine meat pie last night."

"My wife told me that Mrs. Hull feared you would give the job to Mrs. Ralston."

"I was thinking about it. She is younger than Mrs. Hull, and I thought she could get around better," the Vicar confessed. "But Mrs. Hull has dug in and done stuff even Miranda hasn't done in a couple of months."

"Lady Branstoke told me she used to come around to help Mrs. Jones in the garden."

The vicar nodded. "And in her still room as well."

James paused and tilted his head for a moment. "Would she know the recipe for the pennyroyal abortifacient?"

His brow furrowed. "Probably," he said slowly. "It is most likely in one of Miranda's herbal journals."

"Do you know if Mrs. Hall can read?"

"Yes, she can. At one time, when she was young, she was a governess. I heard her and Faith talking about that when Faith was thinking of answering advertisements for governesses. Gave her lots of advice. Now you've got me wondering if she made the tisane for Miss Inglewood." His brows furrowed together as his lips compressed, and he turned to walk back into the house.

James caught his arm. "Easy. No sense running off with worries and assumptions. That will make you no better than those who come to you with their suspicions of Mrs. Jones."

The vicar stopped, his expression crumbling. "There is truth in what you say." He ran a hand through his thinning hair. "But I just want to know!"

"As does everyone else. We'll go together. Let me lead the conversation."

"All right, Sir James. Now that you brought my head around, I hope my wild thoughts are wrong."

They found Mrs. Hull cleaning the shelves in the vicar's study, humming a tuneless song as she worked.

"Mrs. Hull? …Excuse me, Mrs. Hull?" the vicar said, striving to get her attention.

The woman jumped. "Oh!" she said as she turned around. "Oh, vicar, you gave me such a fright, so in my head I be dustin'," she said with a merry smile. "And me hummin' when I know I cain't carry a tune in a bucket," she added with a laugh. "Oh, and hello to you, too, Sir James. I didn't see you there." She curtsied hastily. "Is there somethin' I can do fur you gentlemen?"

"Yes, Mrs. Hull," James said, stepping further into the room. "I would like to know more about Mrs. Jones' herbals. The vicar said he didn't pay much attention to the herbals, but said you often helped her and you might be able to answer some of my questions."

"Yes, I did, so I rightly guess I know more than anyone."

"Can we talk? Vicar, if you'll take your seat behind the

desk, Mrs. Hull and I can then sit here, in your visitor chairs… Excellent," he said as everyone settled in place.

"As no doubt rumor has shared, I was with Mrs. Jones when she died and heard her last words."

"Aye, sar," Mrs. Hull said.

"One of her last words was *pennyroyal*. It sounded like she was telling someone not to use pennyroyal. She said: *No Pennyroyal. Stop stop.* Do you have any notion what she might have meant by that?"

"No pennyroyal. Stop stop," Mrs. Hull repeated softly to herself, her brow furrowing in thought. She shook her head and looked up at first James, then the vicar. "No, I can't say as I do. What I do know is Mrs. Jones said even if she had pennyroyal here, she wouldn't give it to her. This was not the first time Miss Inglewood had been with child, you know," she said with a knowing look.

The gentlemen exchanged looks. "No, Mrs. Hull, I didn't know that," James said softly.

Mrs. Hull nodded sagely. "And it were less than a year ago, too. Mrs. Jones said she had given her the pennyroyal the first time—"

"No," protested the vicar. "My Miranda wouldn't do that."

Mrs. Hull stared at him for a long moment. "I'm sorry, vicar, but you are wrong. She did. But she told me she couldn't do it again, and so she also told Miss Inglewood. That young lady came to visit—I guess it was a week before she died—Miss Inglewood, that be, not Mrs. Jones. She told her she didn't have any, which was true. She said pennyroyal is too strong and it would be too hard on Miss Inglewood's body a second time. She could die or at least become sickly. Told her even if she had the herb, she wouldn't give her any.

Miss Inglewood started screaming at her then, something awful, and ran out of the rectory."

"Do you know for a fact that there is no pennyroyal in Mrs. Jones' stillroom?" James asked her.

"Are you accusing Mrs. Jones of lying?" Mrs. Hull demanded, clearly affronted.

James let a ghost of a smile touch his lips. He liked Mrs. Hull's loyalty. "No; however, sometimes people forget or misplace things. And I imagine it would be easy to do that in a stillroom."

"Humph," Mrs. Hull grunted as she looked at him side-eyed. Then she appeared to relax a little. "I believed her, and I think folks who knew her would take her word. But truthfully, I cain't say. I ain't been in that stillroom for nigh on a month. Haven't had a reason to as there's so much to do in the gardens, planting and weeding, and not much yet available to harvest this time of year."

"Thank you, Mrs. Hull. When you get the opportunity, I would request you check her stillroom."

"For what?"

"For anything out of the ordinary."

While James visited the vicar, Cecilia and her maid, Sarah, walked down into the village. Cecilia didn't have a decided destination. She was walking for inspiration, and intuition told her where to go. The villagers were, by nature, friendly and always up for listening to the latest scrap of gossip. Gossip wasn't Cecilia's favored occupation; however, she owned it could aid in investigations—particularly in villages seemingly ruled by gossip.

They walked past the pub. The door stood propped open, and from the dark interior, she heard the murmur of voices, but she was not wont to look for answers in the pub in the morning when only those who lived to imbibe dwelled there during the day.

As they walked past the pub, Cecilia detected the smell of bread baking. It wafted to them on a light morning breeze from the bakery two buildings further down the road. The old Tudor building had a stone-walled ground floor and a wattle and daub first floor that jutted out over the lower level, shading the door and display window below.

"I think a nice warm bun might be a fine way to start our morning, don't you, Sarah?" Cecilia suggested, steering her maid toward the building.

Sarah's eyes lit up. "Definitely, milady."

"Lady Aldrich told me the baker makes good teething biscuits for the little ones. She purchased biscuits for Charlotte here until her cook devised a biscuit recipe very similar to the baker's."

Sarah made a face. "Babies make such a mess with those biscuits, leaving mushy bits everywhere."

"I know; however, if it helps Hugh to get his teeth in, I won't mind the extra cleaning he requires."

"Just wait until he gets it in your hair and on yourself."

Cecilia laughed. "I shall look forward to it!"

"Ugh!" Sarah returned.

There were two other village women in the bakery when they entered. They moved back to allow her immediate access to the baker; however, Cecilia waved them back into her position. "I just arrived. Please, go ahead. I need to look around and decide what I want," she told them with a warm smile.

The women looked disconcerted; however, they did as she asked.

Cecilia saw loaves of bread on the shelves along the wall and different types of biscuits and muffins on the shelf in front of Mrs. Rutledge, the baker. A young girl of thirteen or fourteen years came out of the back with a large, wooden paddle laden with more loaves of bread for the shelves.

"The buns should be done now, too, Summer. Mustn't let them burn."

"No, Mama. I'll get them straight away," the young girl said, retreating to the back room with her paddle.

When the women before her had finished their purchases and turned to leave, Mrs. Rutledge reached out her hands toward Cecilia, motioning her closer. "Lady Branstoke! You should not have waited!"

Cecilia laughed as she shook her head in denial. "I was not always a titled *Lady*. For eight years I was married to a merchant. I am no better than anyone else."

"Oh! And how is it you are now married to Sir James?" Mrs. Rutledge asked, her face bright with inquisitiveness.

Cecilia belatedly realized she should never have mentioned her first marriage, for Mrs. Rutledge was now on the hunt for information she could pass on to others. "He died, and a year later, I met and married Sir James," Cecilia said simply, hoping to divert more questions about her. "Lady Aldrich told me you make some biscuits that are perfect for a teething baby. Do you have any today?"

"I have four left. They are about a week old; however, these biscuits last at least a month if kept away from bugs."

"I should like to get one for my son, Hugh, to see how he takes to them."

"Is he starting to fuss and drool?" Mrs. Rutledge asked.

"Yes."

She nodded wisely. "How old is he now? Six months?"

"Almost. Mrs. Jones gave me a salve for his gums, which I am almost out of. I do need to find something else to help him."

"Right shame about Mrs. Jones. Fallen down that cliff. — Didn't you find her?"

"Sir James did."

"Is it true she were still alive when he went down the cliff to her?" Mrs. Rutledge leaned forward across the sales counter to ask.

"Yes, though she passed soon after," Cecilia told her.

"Did she say why she done it?"

Cecilia frowned. "Done it? Done what?"

"Why she kilt herself," Mrs. Rutledge said, rocking back on her heels.

"Where did you get the idea she killed herself, Mrs. Rutledge? She did not kill herself; the inquest jury was unanimous at that."

She shook her head. "They would say that with the vicar there. Everyone knows she gave that horrid potion to Miss Inglewood to rid herself of the babe she bore."

Astonished at the depth of belief the baker held as to Mrs. Jones' culpability, Cecilia's mouth fell open as she placed her hands on her hips. She drew herself up, as if she could make her diminutive self taller.

"Mrs. Rutledge, I must protest. Mrs. Jones turned down her request for a potion and had none of the ingredients in her house. I am horrified at the gossip being spread to that effect."

Mrs. Rutledge looked uncomfortable, her lower lip pouting forward. "But she did take her own life. Why would she do that if she were not guilty of something like killing Miss Inglewood?"

"Mrs. Rutledge," Cecilia began again with a calmness she was far from feeling, "Mrs. Jones did not commit suicide. I saw her position down the cliff, and it was not the position of a person who has committed suicide," she said emphatically. "You must tell whoever is speaking these untruths to stop. A better topic for gossip would be to know who is trying to defame Mrs. Jones and what would be their reasons. Are they the ones who acquired the pennyroyal Miss Inglewood took?"

Mrs. Rutledge's shoulders rolled back. Cecilia swore she could almost see the new possibilities for gossip shift through her mind.

Behind her, another villager entered the bakery shop. Cecilia recognized her as the stable owner's wife, Mrs. Broadbank. "Did you say 'pennyroyal'? Isn't that a type of mint?" the woman asked.

Cecilia turned toward her. "I wouldn't know about that," she admitted. "However, pennyroyal can be highly poisonous."

She scowled. "Poisonous? Are you certain?"

"Yes!" Cecilia returned. "It is one of those plants that can have healing properties, but has to be treated carefully, or it is a poison."

Mrs. Broadbank frowned. "I shall have to tell my Marty."

"And why is that?" Cecilia asked.

"She told me it was merely a mint, like one would make tea with."

"Who is Marty?" Cecilia asked.

"My daughter, Martha," Mrs. Broadbank said.

"Is she acquainted with Miss Inglewood?" Cecilia asked.

"She was, all the young people know each other, even if they don't socialize together. I don't believe she was a close friend of Miss Inglewood; her parents wouldn't have allowed it."

"Yes, she was," said a small voice from almost behind Mrs. Rutledge. Summer came around her mother.

"How can you know that, Summer?" asked her mother.

"Because Marty, and Gussie, and Miss Georgia met once a week if the weather were nice to talk of boys and clothes and such. Sometimes they let me come, too. Georgia gave me this dress when it was too small for her," Summer said, pulling the skirt of the dress out from behind her enveloping apron.

Mrs. Rutledge frowned. "I thought I told you to stay away from her. She was no better than she ought to be," her mother reproached her.

"No, Mama," Summer countered. "She was friendly and nice to everyone."

Her mother laughed coarsely. "I'm sure she was."

"She was nice to me. And I helped her, and that's why she gave me this dress."

"How did you help her?" her mother asked, her voice now low and her expression like a thunderstorm about to break.

Summer backed up a step, her face draining of color as she looked up at her mother. "Just…just little stuff. –Umm, like the time I found a handkerchief she lost once, and I washed it and pressed it before I gave it back to her. She was impressed with my attention to do that."

Cecilia was certain the girl had done more than find a lost

handkerchief, but her mother's manner scared her from relating more. She wished she could talk to her without her mother around.

Cecilia purchased the baby biscuit and four sweet buns from Mrs. Rutledge, then she and Sarah left the bakery.

"Milady," Sarah whispered after the door closed behind them, "I've never seen a person change so swiftly as that Mrs. Rutledge did from the nice, smiling lady to the angry-faced woman she became when she addressed her daughter."

"I know. And by Summer's expression, she's seen that anger before. It frightened her. I hope she does not punish Summer for speaking up."

"I didn't get the feeling it was because she spoke; it was more because she talked about Miss Inglewood having friends and Summer doing favors for her."

"This has been an interesting morning. Let's go to the drygoods store to see about fabric for new infant gowns for Hugh and what they have to say about Miss Inglewood and Mrs. Jones there." Cecilia said. "It seems everyone has an opinion."

The drygoods store was busy, but not with shoppers looking at the different products that could be found in the store. They stood in a queue before a clerk's tall desk, where Mr. Sandiford—dressed like a city clerk in a neat brown suit and waistcoat—sat writing. He took payments for what was immediately available in the store and wrote what must be ordered from larger market towns in a ledger book.

Mrs. Sandiford, speaking with one of the customers in the queue, broke off her conversation when she saw Cecilia enter the store. "Lady Branstoke, to what do we owe the pleasure of your commerce?" she declared.

Cecilia, looking around at the store's merchandise, slowly brought her gaze to Mrs. Sandiford. "I beg your pardon if I stare at everything I see here in your store!" she said. "You seem to have a bit of everything."

Mrs. Sandiford laughed indulgently. "We have a little of a lot."

Cecilia looked at her quizzically.

"What I mean is, we do not carry many multiples of items. We prefer to show what we can get easily and take orders for what our customers want," she explained. "With the Folkestone, Canterbury, Maidstone, and London markets so close, we generally fill orders in less than two days. We do sell the merchandise we have on hand and immediately order replacements—or order what has become the newest trend."

Cecilia nodded. "Wisely done."

"It seems to work for us," Mrs. Sandiford said, rocking back on her heels, while clasping her hands before her. "So what brings you here today?"

"Fabric for infant gowns," Cecilia said. "Our son, Hugh, is rapidly outgrowing his newborn gowns."

"And you'd like to make him new ones," the woman said.

"Not me; a member of my staff has volunteered. If I tried to sew, I'd have the material all stained from blood due to pinpricks. Do you have any plain, light-colored muslin or lawn that we can consider?"

Mrs. Sandiford laughed. "Let's see what we have left."

She guided Cecilia and Sarah to a far wall where fabric lay folded. She ran a finger up and down the shelves until she spotted a thin fold of white. She pulled it out. "Och, I thought I'd found what you desire; however, this one has small embroidered flowers. Not what I suspect you want for a baby boy."

Cecilia touched the cloth. "It is very pretty, and the weight is good, but you are correct. Not for my Hugh. You have nothing else?"

Mrs. Sandiford looked back at her shelves. "Not at the moment. The plain fabric sells quickly. I am expecting twenty ells of white, pale-blue, and a cream-colored fabric, amongst other fabrics, late today when the local carter returns from his London pickups. I can set some aside for you if you tell me how much you want and tomorrow have Gussie bring it to you at the Park."

"Who is Gussie?"

"Augusta—Gussie, as everyone addresses her—is our eldest daughter. She is over there," Mrs. Sandiford said, pointing to a neatly dressed young woman wearing a blue dress and a pale gray full dress covering apron. She appeared to be assisting a bent old woman with getting an item off a shelf.

Perfect! Cecilia thought. To Mrs. Sandiford, she ticked off on her fingers what she would like in fabric. "An infant's dress doesn't take much fabric. I'd like an ell of pale blue, an ell of the cream you mentioned, and four ells of white—if taking that much won't leave you too short for other customers and their orders."

Mrs. Sandiford shook her head. "It shan't," she assured Cecilia. "...Lady Branstoke," she began tentatively, "might I ask you a question?"

"Of course," Cecilia returned.

"Mrs. Jones," she began, "did she suffer much?"

Her question surprised and pleased Cecilia. Hers was not a ghoulish rumor-mongering question.

"I'm afraid I can't say with certainty; however, judging by the position I saw her in, and what my husband has told me—for he was next to her when she passed—I would have to say yes, she did."

"Oh dear," said Mrs. Sandiford softly, her expression shifting to sadness. "I was afraid that would be the case. Thank you for being honest and not offering me a sugar-dusted answer." She compressed her lips tightly together for a moment, then shook off the sadness. "You know, there are those who believe she provided the pennyroyal tea, which undoubtedly killed Miss Inglewood—not that story of iliac passion," she declared, standing straighter. "Only one person ordered pennyroyal tea through us, and that was Mrs. Hester."

"The housekeeper for the Inglewood family?"

"The very same, and naught but three days before the Inglewood girl died."

CHAPTER 8

MISS GEORGIA'S COTERIE

"You were gone a long while in the village today," observed Sir James as he handed his wife her preprandial later that day as they gathered in the morning room to await dinner.

Cecilia nodded. "Yes. It was a most instructive day. Though we have lived here at Summerworth Park for the past two years, we have not taken the opportunity to get to know the village as we might."

"I should say we have been rather busy," James observed as he sat down on the couch with her. He casually crossed his legs and leaned back into the corner of the couch to make it easier to converse.

"I suppose so; however, even our staff is not as well-known in the village."

James inclined his head in acknowledgement. "We tend to send our people directly to the market towns for what we need rather than use the services we might find in our own village."

"I don't imagine even our footmen or grooms visit the

97

village pub regularly, as we have ale readily available here for free. We need to make a better effort to be part of the community."

"There is merit in what you say. If we were more visible, it might make it easier for us to investigate what happened to Mrs. Jones."

"Hmmm. Perhaps, however, I can use the village not knowing us to our advantage. The village thrives on gossip, as you may have found out."

James snorted a laugh. "Yes. And people are quick to make up what they don't know."

"And they don't know us. I saw a certain avarice in the baker's attention to me to learn more about my history that she might be the first to let fall of it to others. I might use that desire to my advantage."

James frowned. "I don't like the idea of you calling down gossip upon yourself."

"Do not be concerned. I will not dwell on Mr. Waddley. I'm trying to decide when and to whom I should reveal my grandfather's identity."

James chuckled. "Depending on the folklore surrounding the Duke of Cheney, that could be to your disadvantage as well as advantage."

"With the passing of time, his exploits have acquired a romantic patina."

"If you say so." He shook his head. "However, highway-man-to-duke tales have more grit, danger, and criminal aspects than romantic tales."

"To some, he was the Robin Hood of his time."

"If one didn't acknowledge that the poor he shared with was himself," James returned drily.

"Not totally," Cecilia argued with a smile.

James tossed off the rest of his drink. "You know his stories far better than I."

"Yes, and bringing a bit of my grandfather's stories into conversations might be good."

"So long as he and the duchess never journey here to visit."

"Nonsense. He'd only laugh at whatever tales got back to him, thinking it all a great hum."

James laughed. "I'll not argue with you any longer. So what have you learned today?"

"Most seem to believe Mrs. Jones gave Georgia a fatal dose of pennyroyal and then committed suicide out of remorse. I have detected a kind of comfort with that solution," she said, her brows furrowing as she recalled the manners of those she talked with.

"I concur; some have even taken to approaching the vicar saying they know that is what happened but they won't argue against her having a shriven burial. They have upset the vicar. As Mr. McCurdy is going to be doing repairs at the church, I have requested he intervene if others come to say these same words to the vicar."

"So ridiculous when we know the jury found Mrs. Jones's death not to be suicide." Cecilia huffed.

"The sense is that the magistrate has painted himself into a corner with his insistence that Georgia died of natural causes, yet he believes Mrs. Jones culpable. He could be part of the rumors flying through the village."

Cecilia's brows rose. "Even when it makes him a liar."

"Even so," James said.

Cecilia nodded. She held out her small glass to James for a refill. He rose to grab the decanter from the sideboard and refilled their glasses. When he had seated himself again, she continued.

"Miss Inglewood was more egalitarian in her friendships than her family would have her be. She was close friends with Augusta Sandiford, the drygoods daughter, and Martha Broadbank. And she let Summer Rutledge trail along with them because she could use her to run errands for her. For some reason that I do not know yet, Mrs. Rutledge was particularly irate at discovering Summer was friends with Miss Inglewood. I was, for a time, quite fearful for Summer."

"You think her mother might have beaten her?" James asked.

"Yes. I have a plan to ask Mrs. Rutledge for more of the baby biscuits for Hugh and some sweet rolls for us. It is my understanding that Summer does her deliveries, which is probably how she began to do errands for Miss Inglewood."

"You intend to befriend the girl?"

"If I can. I also have Augusta Sandiford coming tomorrow to deliver fabric for new clothes for Hugh. I will use that opportunity to get to know her better as well. I think the young people in the village know more about Miss Inglewood than her parents or anyone else. I'm interested to learn if the smith's boys dangled after Miss Inglewood as well. Being twins, there could have been a rivalry between them for Miss Inglewood's affections."

"I wonder if either of them might have been the father of her child."

Cecilia shrugged. "It's possible. I will know more after talking with Summer and Miss Broadbank."

"Excuse me, Sir James, Lady Branstoke, dinner is served," announced Coggins from the doorway.

"Thank you," Sir James said. He rose to his feet and extended his hand toward his wife. "My dear, let's put more conjecture on this mystery aside so we might enjoy a quiet dinner together."

Cecilia smiled up at her husband as he drew her up and tucked her arm in his. "It will be my delight," she said, with a wanton look in her eyes.

Sir James laughed.

THE NEXT MORNING, the youngest scullery maid crept into the morning room. "Pardon, milady, Cook sent me to tell you that Miss Rutledge is in the kitchen with the bakery items you requested," the little maid said. She looked wide-eyed all around her as she spoke, so seldom did she leave the kitchen domain. "Cook said you wished to speak to her when she came today?"

"Yes," Cecilia said, setting aside the London newspaper she'd been reading, and rose from the couch in the morning room. "I'll be there directly," she told the young woman.

She grabbed her shawl from the couch and wrapped it around her, then followed the maid to the kitchen, where she found Summer Rutledge standing by the heavy wood prep table, enjoying a mug of lemonade.

The young girl thrust the mug toward the cook, a look of fear in her eyes when she saw Cecilia approaching.

"Finish your drink, dearie," the cook told her, handing the mug back to her.

"But..." began the girl, looking between the cook and Lady Branstoke.

"Please, finish your drink," Cecilia told her. "That's a dusty walk from the bakery to Summerworth Park. You deserve to refresh yourself." Cecilia watched as the young girl looked again uncertainly between her and the cook, then took the mug back and gulped it down. Cecilia laughed. "Did you like it?"

Summer nodded as she wiped her mouth with the back of her hand. "Yes, milady, and thankee, milady," she said, bobbing two quick curtsies with her answer.

"I'd like to talk with you more about the unfortunate Miss Inglewood. Come, let's go outside to the garden to talk. You can bring your basket with you. I promise not to take up too much of your time so your mother will not fuss," she said with a smile to the young girl.

"I never met Miss Inglewood," Cecilia told her as they entered the garden. "It appeared yesterday that you knew her quite well. Can you tell me about her?"

"Oh, milady, she were so nice and kind to me always—except when I lost one of her messages." Her brow furrowed. "But that's to be expected, right?" She looked up at Cecilia like a puppy that knew it had done wrong.

"What happened?"

"I had a note to take to Mr. Vernon."

"The brewer?" Cecilia asked.

"Yes'm. She cuffed me good when I told her, but after she were so nice and acted as if nothing had happened."

"Did she apologize?" Cecilia asked.

"Oh, no, milady. It were my mistake. I deserved it. But she didn't bear no grudge."

Cecilia compressed her lips together. She had plenty to say about Miss Inglewood's behavior and about what she'd witnessed at the bakery yesterday; however, she knew she would serve the poor girl best by simply listening to her. Time later for taking all parties to task.

"The very next day, she gave me a straw bonnet she didn't want anymore. I fixed it up a bit, and now I wear it to church on Sunday. Even my mother likes it—even if it did come from Miss Georgia."

"Your mother did not like Miss Inglewood."

"No. Said she needed to keep with her own kind. Said no good came of the classes mixing like they be friends when the Lord knew they never could be. That only brought about hurt."

"It sounds like your mother might have spoken from the place of some experience," Cecilia observed.

Summer shrugged. "Miss Georgia, she was friends with all of us in the village. It weren't like there were others of her sort around except for the Viscount, and he's old and a bit stuffy."

"Old?" countered Cecilia in surprise.

"He don't acknowledge none of us, like we don't exist. – La!" she said, laughing. "You should have seen his face when he realized I was trying to give him a message from Miss Georgia. I had the durndest time getting his attention so I could give him the note."

"Who did you take notes to?" Cecilia asked.

"Oh, everyone!" She swung one arm wildly in an arc to encompass her world. "Gussie and Marty a'course as they were her special friends, the Viscount, Mr. Vernon, Jerome Abernathy—though he weren't happy to get one of her notes on account he's sweet on a girl in the next village—and the blacksmithy's twins." She laughed again. "They were so jealous of each other. Miss Georgia told me—confidential-like—that she only sent notes to them on account it was fun to watch them get in fights with each other. That weren't nice, I know, but they'd take off their shirts and git to fightin' and wrestlin', so it were fun to watch. If I were older, I'd wish either Jebus or Josiah Cathcart would pay attention to me. Coo…" she breathed out, a dreamy expression on her thirteen-year-old face.

Cecilia bit back a laugh at the expression. "How did you get the messages you were to deliver? Did you visit her every day?"

"No. She left 'em in the old henhouse."

"Old henhouse?" Cecilia queried.

"Yes, by the abandoned cottage in the earl's woods. The twins fixed the roof of the cottage, and Miss Georgia had us clean up the inside and that's where we met."

"I'd like to see this cottage," Cecilia said. "Can you take me there?"

Summer shook her head. "Oh, no, milady. We made a pact… I've got to get back to the bakery," she said suddenly, her face now twisted with worry. She started to run toward the drive, then stopped and turned back. She curtsied. "Good-bye, milady," she said, then turned and ran down the drive toward the village.

Cecilia watched after her. Likely, the group still met at the old cottage. She would have thought that with the loss of Miss Inglewood, the glue that had held them together, the group would have dissolved. She turned back to the house and pondered how she would approach her conversation with Miss Augusta Sandiford when she delivered the fabric.

AT CECILIA'S REQUEST, Cook set a cold collation in the breakfast parlor for a nuncheon that could be partaken whenever she and James were available. It had been a practice started during their early days of the estate remodel two years ago. Now they frequently continued the practice when they did not know when they might be available to eat. They seldom came to nuncheon at the same time, so it was with surprise and delight that Cecilia entered the small parlor to find James ahead of her, choosing his food. She went to his side and stood on tiptoe to kiss his cheek. He obliged her efforts by bending his head down toward her, then he smiled at her.

"I have news for you," he said.

"As I have for you," Cecilia returned, "but you go first while I get my plate," she said, looking across what the cook had spread out for them this day. It was never the same, depending on what Cook found in the larder that she thought they might enjoy.

"First, Romley told me Mrs. Jones' horse did have painting supplies packed in a satchel slung over the pommel."

"So she had gone to paint," Cecilia said.

"It looks that way. And in another bit of news, Miss Hope Jones has come to Mertonhaugh for her mother's services."

"I'm so glad," Cecilia returned. "Any word about her sister?"

"None as yet; however, I believe the earliest she could possibly arrive is this evening. But overall, I assume it depends on the tides and winds."

Cecilia nodded. She set her plate down on the table. "Just

lemonade for me," she told Daniel as the attending footman poured a glass of wine for Sir James.

"I shall have to go to the rectory this afternoon to pay my respects," she said as she cut her ham slice.

"She is not staying at the rectory," James told her, one of his smirking smiles on his face.

"She's not? Where is she staying? Certainly not at the tavern inn."

"No. She is staying at Mortlake House."

Cecilia's eyes widened as she considered that. "Well, he is her father. But I'm sure that must hurt Mr. Jones' heart."

"I don't know why she is staying there, so I caution you about making assumptions."

"Yes, I know; however, if I am, you know what the biddies of Mertonhaugh will be saying. It is bad enough that talk insists Mrs. Jones committed suicide because she poisoned Miss Inglewood. I've only known Mrs. Jones for two years and know her to be a kind, strong woman who is strong in her beliefs and wouldn't hurt anyone. These people have known her for over twenty years, and yet the minute something unsavory is presented as a possibility, they rush to condemnation. I do not understand it." Cecilia's voice had grown louder and more insistent as she talked. Sir James laid his hand atop hers.

"Easy, love," he counseled in his even manner. "There is agency behind these gossips, I'm certain. We need to discover who and why. It will come out in due time. It always does with gossip such as this."

"I certainly hope so."

"But tell me of your news."

"Summer Rutledge, the baker's daughter, acted as Miss

Inglewood's courier to all her friends and swains in the village. She picked up the notes she was to deliver from an old henhouse."

"An old henhouse!"

"Yes, and your reaction is the same as mine. An old henhouse associated with an abandoned cottage on the earl's estate."

"Hmm. Did you discover where this cottage is?"

"No, and the girl seemed sorry she had said as much as she did. Evidently, it is still in use by Miss Inglewood's associates."

"It should be fairly simple to discover its whereabouts after a discussion with the earl or his steward."

"Yes, but I do not see the reason for haste to do so—unless you believe we might find pennyroyal there."

"Possibly, however, I wouldn't believe so. Their continued gatherings could be innocent gatherings to mourn another's death."

"True."

"Did you discover who was in Miss Inglewood's thrall?"

"Thrall? Interesting, descriptive word and possibly accurate," Cecilia mused with a smile.

"Summer delivered messages to Martha Broadbank, Augusta Sandiform, the Cathcart twins, Mr. Vernon, and... Viscount Kendell."

"The Viscount!"

"Yes. I do wonder about that relationship. A match between them is not out of the realm of acceptability."

"And might be something her parents would encourage, so why the secret notes delivered by another child?"

"Because it was not a connection either took seriously? It was a youthful game?"

"Possibly; however, one would think that with the example of his father, the Viscount might steer away from such potential entanglements. I'll have to see if I can't arrange a discreet word with the viscount."

"I thought you might. This afternoon, if the delivery wagon returns on time from London, I should receive some fabric for Hugh's clothes. Mrs. Sandiford said she would have her daughter deliver it. I will try to speak to her about Miss Inglewood and try to learn more about this group and their meetings."

"I will go by the church today to see how McCurdy is getting on with his work. I'll see if I can get a feeling on how the vicar is doing," James said, setting his serviette down on the table. "I hope to be back in time for tea. I missed my time with Hugh yesterday. I don't want to miss two days in a row."

Cecilia grinned. "That would not be good, else he might forget you."

"Minx," James countered as he walked out of the room.

"MISS SANDIFORD! OVER HERE!" Cecilia called out when she saw Miss Sandiford approach the servants' entrance. She'd been enjoying her afternoon tea from the shady back terrace, hoping to see the young woman approach.

The package Augusta Sandiford carried looked unwieldy, more than Cecilia would have considered for five ells of fabric. The young woman looked burdened, her brown hair curling damply around the edges of her bonnet, a sheen on her forehead.

"Daniel," Cecilia called out to the footman standing by the

terrace door, "please take that package from Miss Sandiford and put it on the bench, then fetch her a glass of lemonade."

Augusta Sandiford looked up, startled, when Daniel reached for the bundle she carried. "Oh, yes. Thank you!" she managed and slowly released her clasp as she stared at the tall, blond footman. She stood stock still, watching him. When he turned to go into the house to fetch the lemonade, she remembered herself and turned toward Cecilia, a blush staining her cheeks beyond what her exertions had given her.

Cecilia pressed her lips against a laugh. Daniel often had that effect on young ladies, and Miss Sandiford was at the right age to take note of his attributes. "Come sit here with me while we wait for Daniel to return," she told the young woman. "That was quite a large bundle you carried here. I can't believe my five ells are that bulky."

"No, my lady," Miss Sandiford said as she slid into the chair across from Cecilia. "In the shipment we received yesterday was a beautiful, blue-figured heavy cotton that Mama swore would match your eyes. She sent it on with your order to see if you might be interested—no obligation, of course," she hurriedly added.

Cecilia laughed. "Your mother is an astute businesswoman. I am interested in seeing the material. I haven't had a new outfit in over a year, and though I have lost the weight of carrying Hugh, none of my old clothes quite fit me anymore as I should like."

"I'll show you, then," Miss Sandiford said eagerly. "I agreed with mother," she continued as she rose to go to the bench. "The fabric will look wonderful on you." She pulled on the string holding the wrapped parcel in brown paper. The paper crinkled as the string fell away. Miss Sandiford quickly pushed the paper aside to reveal a beautiful dark-blue fabric. "There are ten ells here. Mother also said you did not have to take it all if you did not need that much." She picked up the folded material and brought it to the terrace table.

Cecilia reached out to touch the fabric. It was a beautiful color, though perhaps a trifle darker than her eyes; it would highlight them nicely—something James would like. "I do like this material, though at the moment, I have no idea what I should like to make of it. Too many ideas to settle on one," she said with a laugh as she felt the thickness and texture of the fabric. "I will take it all."

"But you don't even know the cost!" Miss Sandiford protested.

"No matter. A woman doesn't often come across a fabric that is so suited to her as I feel this is to me. Your mother is a genius."

The young woman nodded eagerly, then blushed as she saw Daniel come out of the house bearing a large mug of lemonade.

"Miss Sandiford," he said courteously as he placed the mug before her.

Cecilia raised her brows. Daniel did not habitually address their guests; that he had called her by name was most singular. While Daniel was studiously polite, Cecilia saw he looked longer at Miss Sandiford than was his wont to do. *Interesting*, she thought as he walked back to his station by the terrace doors.

"Miss Sandiford, I shall have Daniel bring payment to the store by the end of the week."

"Oh, there is no rush for payment, Lady Branstoke. Father

made a ledger page in his account book for Summerworth Park."

"I appreciate that; however, I prefer to see my debts are paid promptly. You see, my father lived on credit, and I found it embarrassing, especially as he so seldom paid on his accounts. –But I don't wish to talk about bills and such. I should like to learn more about Miss Inglewood."

"Georgia?" Miss Sandiford said.

"Yes, Miss Georgia Inglewood."

Miss Sandiford looked decidedly uncomfortable with that topic of conversation. Cecilia knew she needed to find a way to calm her fears. "So young to die," she said. "I heard she was not one to snub those who by birth might be considered a lower class."

Miss Sandiford's expression perked up. "Yes. Much to her parents' dismay."

"So I have been led to believe," Cecilia said.

"It's true, my lady. She was fun to be around! –My mother thought her too wild."

"Did she forbid you to have anything to do with her?"

"No, Mother is too wise for that. This is a small village, and our mercantile is where everyone comes."

"Did you consider her wild?" Cecilia asked.

"With the boys in the village, mayhap," Miss Sandiford said after considering a moment.

Cecilia nodded. "Yes, getting with child does speak to a wild recklessness."

"Georgia said she had to experience life before she went to London for the season next year, else she'd be considered a country bumpkin. I told her having intimate relations with the boys here would not give her town bronze, but she laughed at me."

"Do you know who the father of her baby was?"

"No, and I don't think she did either, though she *claimed* it was the viscount."

"Did she? I hadn't heard that. To whom did she say that?"

"To Martha and me, the last time we saw her. She said if she couldn't shed the baby, she would make the viscount responsible. At least he had rank."

"I'm sorry, Miss Sandiford; however, she sounds callous for the way she talked of getting rid of a new life. I can understand circumstances where it is warranted; however, her attitude makes me shiver. I can't imagine losing my Hugh," Cecilia said, losing her sympathetic tone.

Miss Sandiford sighed. "You would have to have known Georgia to understand. She was fun, like I said, but she thought only of today. She said, 'Tomorrow can go to bloody hell' —excuse my language, my lady, but that is what she said on many a day."

"Do you know why Mrs. Jones would not give her the pennyroyal this time?"

Miss Sandiford shook her head. "Not rightly, though her refusal sure made Georgia mad. We thought the vicar's wife had gotten more puritanical because she got herself with child again."

Cecilia shook her head. "I learned from Mrs. Aldrich and Mrs. Hull that Mrs. Jones said a second usage of pennyroyal would likely kill her or make her have long-term consequences. Pennyroyal is a plant that can as easily kill the person taking it as the baby they carried. It had likely already done some injury to Miss Inglewood's insides. The recipe for the tisane must be followed exactly and with great care."

"Recipe?" Miss Sandiford asked, her eyes wide.

"Yes. The quantity used in the tisane needed to be precisely measured."

The color drained from Miss Sandiford's face.

"I didn't know that. I suspect Georgia didn't either—or, if she did, she didn't believe that was the case." She pushed the mug away from her and hurriedly got to her feet. "I must go. Mama will be wondering where I am." She curtsied. "Thank you for the lemonade," she said and turned to run off the terrace and back to the village.

Cecilia watched her for a moment, then turned to Daniel. "Discreetly follow her, if you can, and let me know where she goes and who she sees."

"You don't think she will go home?"

"No. She will run to tell someone what I told her about Mrs. Jones. I'd like to know who that is."

CHAPTER 9

BEER AND ALE

James acknowledged that the few times he'd been in the Mortlake Brewery, he had not looked at its workings. After his conversation with Lord Mortlake, he was curious to learn more about its operation—and more about Haydon Vernon, the brewmaster, and his housekeeper's nephew. Mr. Vernon had been one of the people who had been in Miss Inglewood's orbit. He'd see whether he could learn more about their relationship.

Built of Kentish stone alongside the River Merton, a tributary of the River Medway, the three-story rectangular building commanded its location at the far end of the village. Tall, arched windows dominated the east end of the building, while on the west end, a wide stone chimney billowed smoke from fireplaces lit at various levels. Even if one did not know the building housed a brewery, the overwhelming smell of beer and barley in the air would reveal the building's purpose.

When Sir James entered the building, he looked up. The building was open to the roof in the center, with the U-shaped floors above looking down to the ground floor. Open vats of liquid on the upper floors appeared in various stages of beer production, some with steam drifting up. Sluices and leather hoses connected the vats on the different levels to each other.

James stopped a man carrying a ladle attached to a long stick. "Is Mr. Vernon here today?"

The man jerked his head upward. "Top floor, checkin' the grind, sar." He used his ladle stick to point to a broad oak staircase. "You can go up that way if'n ya wants to see him."

James thanked the man and climbed the stairs, stopping occasionally to look at the work of the men in the areas he passed. From behind him came the heavy tread of a broad-shouldered man carrying a large grain sack on his shoulder. James stepped to the side to let him pass by.

The stairs ended near one of the hearths in the massive chimney. A soot-streaked man shoveled hot coals from the hearth to under a vat to heat the water another man pumped in. He paused a moment to look over Sir James as he dragged the back of his arm across his sweating forehead.

"Mr. Vernon?" James asked.

"That way," the man said, indicating a walkway on the left.

Sir James nodded and continued down that way. The top floor was hotter than the other floors, and made only bearable by the open roof windows. The man who'd passed him carrying the sack of grain came back the other way, touching his forelock as he passed him. James was struck with admiration that everywhere he looked, the men worked. No casual conversations or pausing to rest and lean against railings occurred. He mentioned that observation to Mr. Vernon when he came up to him by the barley grinder.

"Yes, sir. I wish I could say it were really a good work

ethic, but in honesty, it's a might more complicated than that," Mr. Vernon said ruefully. He brushed a lock of his burnished dark-red hair off his forehead. "It's getting too hot to make beer. Today's the last day of beer brewing till autumn."

"I thought beer making was a year-round industry," James said.

Mr. Vernon shook his head. "Nay. Not in our part of England. From tomorrow until October, we'll only be making ale. Making ale is not as complex as making beer, and I'll not need as many workers. No one wants to be let go for four months, but that's a sad fact of the brewery business... Lord Mortlake said I might see you," Mr. Vernon said, canting his head to the side quizzically.

"He told me he's planning a major brewery expansion," James said by way of explanation.

Mr. Vernon's mouth quirked to the side. "Yes. A moment, please. Silas, take that grist to Tommy to mash. He should have that water at temperature by now." He pulled James to the wall to give Silas room to maneuver his large woven basket of ground grain to the vat of heated water at the end of the walkway by the staircase.

"By your expression, I gather you are not enamored with Mortlake's plans," James observed drily.

"We should expand," Mr. Vernon said, walking with James toward the stairs, "just not as he plans with the expansion across the river and expecting me to run both. Beer and ale need managin'. I can't go runnin' hither and yon."

"You'll have to promote someone."

Mr. Vernon laughed. "Aye. But who? But that's a problem for another day; he don't even have plans yet from that fancy architect he hired."

"I told him I'm planning to build an oast house at Summerworth Park," James said.

"Good! Some days, the Mortlake oast house can't keep up with demand. If he wanted to expand, that is what he should have expanded first, that's what I say. His oast house also needs to dry grain for other purposes, and sometimes that causes delays for us."

"So you would buy from me?"

"Definitely, if your product's to the right dryness," Mr. Vernon said as they started down the stairs.

James nodded thoughtfully. "That helps solidify my plans for sooner rather than later."

They stopped for a moment on the next floor down, and Mr. Vernon watched his workers draw the wort off from the vat on the floor above. "You want a bright and clear wort to use," he told James. He nodded as he saw the liquid. "Looks good," he said, then motioned James that they could continue down the stairs.

"At this second level, they'll add the hops and yeast."

"What conditions prevent the addition of hops?" James asked, knowing that was the crucial difference between beer and ale.

"The hops brew has to come to blood temperature within a certain timeframe. If it takes too long to cool, the taste will be off."

"Blood temperature?" James queried.

Mr. Vernon laughed. "That's what we call it. The same temperature as our blood."

"Ah," James nodded.

"Speaking of blood," Mr. Vernon said as they reached the

ground floor, "I was surprised at how little blood was on Mrs. Jones." He slid a look toward James.

"One could hardly see the blood on her for all the chalk dust," James said. "But, in truth, her injuries were primarily internal, from what Dr. Patterson said… I expect that is why she lived as long as she did." His voice softened as he thought of Mrs. Jones.

Mr. Vernon's lips compressed. He took a deep breath as he shook his head. "Poor woman. Do you think someone pushed her?" he asked tentatively.

"What do you think?" James countered.

He quickly shook his head, frowning. "No. I assume the ground gave way beneath her."

"But that raises the question, why was she so close to the edge as to be in danger of crumbling chalk?"

Mr. Vernon took another deep breath and stared off into the brewery, then he looked back at James. "Fear," he suggested.

James nodded. "That is what Lady Branstoke and I believe, especially after having found her brooch in the grass on the other side of the meadow."

"I remember you said that at the inquest. All that makes sense to me," Mr. Vernon said, still watching the activities of his staff. Then he turned toward James. "Come this way and I'll treat you to a taste of our latest brews."

He led James to a small bar. "No one would want to hurt Mrs. Jones," he continued as he drew off a mug of beer from the large cask over the bar.

"Some people blame Mrs. Jones for Miss Inglewood's death." He accepted the mug from Mr. Vernon.

"That is ridiculous," Mr. Vernon said quickly as he drew

off a mug for himself. "Everyone knows she refused to give her that tea she wanted."

"True. But did she later relent?"

Mr. Vernon shrugged. "I wouldn't think so. Miss Inglewood asked everyone to get her some pennyroyal."

"You don't agree with the inquest findings that she died from iliac passion?"

Mr. Vernon gave a disgusted look as he shook his head. "No, nor do I feel she committed suicide. She was much too full of herself to do that. No, we all got her some of that plant she wanted. That's what I believe, and she didn't have the right recipe."

"You said 'we all.' I've heard that she had a coterie of followers and you were part of that group."

Mr. Vernon drew back. "Me? Hardly, though she kept trying, always sending me notes. She were pretty and lively enough to catch a man's interest, in God's truth," he said with a sideways smile. "But she were also too free with her sweet words and promises. I learned that fast enough," he declared harshly. "But I did get her that rotted plant. I could hardly not."

James thought the swift change from smile to harsh words interesting. "I take it from what you say that she tried to capture your interest?"

"And the interest of any manor boy!" He took another drink of his beer, still frowning.

Noting Mr. Vernon's heightened emotions, James thought it time to divert the subject slightly if he wished to learn more from Mr. Vernon.

"Do you know anything about a hut in the Mortlake forest where she and others gathered?"

Vernon nodded. "The old gamekeeper's hut. It's close to the southeast corner of the Inglewood property. Le Grange complained about the Mortlake gamekeeper living so close to his property because the man raised chickens and they were always squawking and getting into the Inglewood manor garden. To keep peace, Mortlake had a new hut built at the other end of his forest."

James mused on how everyone seemed to placate the Inglewoods. He wondered why, but said, "And Miss Inglewood claimed the hut as her private club."

The brewer nodded. "She invited me to meet her there on several occasions. I was not interested."

"Do you have any idea why your name has been suggested as a possible father of her unborn child?"

"What? Me? No! No!" he said hastily. He downed the rest of his beer and wiped his mouth on his sleeve. "I was always pleasant enough with her in public. We all were. Had to be. Squire Inglewood could make life embarrassing and difficult for anyone he thought did not worship the ground his daughter walked on."

James frowned. "What would he do?"

Haydon Veron threw up his hands. "Anything! Everything! –But I can only share my experience." He scowled. "Our good magistrate made up a reason to throw me into his gaol overnight, told others I was a libertine. He even suggested during a visit to the town tavern that I had clap."

"What!" James protested.

Mr. Vernon gave a tight laugh. "That one was a mistake on his part. Lord Mortlake and Dr. Patterson heard the story and went to see Inglewood. I don't know what was said; however,

I was released, and all the more vile of Inglewood's accusations stopped."

"I should hope so," James declared.

Mr. Vernon nodded. "Lord Mortlake said that rumor would be death for the Mortlake Brewery if it got bandied about far and wide. He would not tolerate that."

"I would imagine not! One would suppose a magistrate would be above lies."

Mr. Vernon sighed. "One would, yes."

THE SHEEP'S Head Tavern was not an old building in Mertonhaugh, as the original structure had burned down some twenty years past. The tavern stood out from the Kentish stone of most of the village with its clean, symmetrical Georgian design and white stucco exterior. Inside, however, the new pub owner, Mr. Gilbert Hopkins, had disavowed the open Georgian style as too uninviting. He'd paneled the walls with dark oak, expanded the fireplace, and placed settles around it to encourage customers to relax and stay awhile.

For this reason, James considered Mr. Hopkins an intelligent and shrewd man who saw more and said less. He had been summoned to the inquest jury and had sat to the side, his thick arms crossed, resting on his ample stomach.

After leaving the Mortlake Brewery, James walked to the Sheep's Head for a chat with Mr. Hopkins. A few of the older residents were gathered at tables, eating their midday meal from wooden bowls. He nodded to them as he threaded his way through the empty tables to the bar.

Mr. Hopkins approached him. "Ken I git youse a beer, sar?" he asked, rubbing the already clean bar in front of where James stood with the cloth he carried.

"Just ale, Mr. Hopkins," James said as he settled his foot on the iron boot rail near the floor. He leaned his right arm on the bar top. "What did you think of the inquest the other day?" he asked as Mr. Hopkins slid a mug of ale in front of him.

Mr. Hopkins frowned. He leaned his elbows on the bar. "Squire Inglewood ken be a bit officious, wantin' everything to go his way."

"Why do you suppose he wanted Mrs. Jones' death ruled a suicide?"

"'Cause he were afraid that chit of his committed suicide," said Mrs. Hopkins, interrupting as she entered the bar area from the kitchen. A handsome woman, she was probably ten years younger than her husband, with gray only beginning to visit the dark-brown hair she wore in a tight bun. "Shows he didn't know his own daughter well. I tell you, sar, if she couldn't get rid of the babe, that tart woulda found a way to turn it to advantage. That she would," she said, her voice rife with disgust. "Now, can I bring you a hot, fresh pastie, Sir James?" the woman added.

James laughed. "You were not sympathetic to the young woman?"

She shook her head. "Not that one. A witch she were, and she had her parents, her brother, and others in the village feelin' beholden to her, if you can imagine that."

"Beholden?" James asked, his brows coming together in a questioning frown. "Why do you say *beholden*?"

She flung her hands up. "She had people fallin' over each other to help her. They thought her clever—too clever to ever be wrong, and that's a fact. Now, can I git you a pastie or not?" she demanded, her hands on her hips.

James laughed slightly and told her yes, she could. He pulled up a stool and sat down.

"Your wife is not behind in her opinions," James observed to Mr. Hopkins when his wife went back into the kitchen.

"No, not that one. I hope she didn't give you a distaste for her, bein' too forward like that, Sir James."

"Not at all!" James assured him. "Reminds me of my wife, Lady Branstoke. The two of them would get along."

Hopkins' eyes widened. "Kind of youse, Sir James—"

James laughed at his expression. He'd nearly forgotten that in this village there was decided class bias, engendered, he suspected, more by Squire Inglewood than anyone else in the village—including the Earl of Mortlake! "My wife was a widow when I met her. Her first husband was a merchant trader."

"But I heard she is the granddaughter of a duke!" Mrs. Hopkins said, sliding a pewter plate with a pastie in front of him.

"She is," James said, eyeing the aromatic pastie. "This smells delicious, Mrs. Hopkins."

Mrs. Hopkins frowned. "Excuse me for asking, Sir James, but how'd she come to marry a merchant?"

"That is a complicated story," James said, thinking of how the arranged marriage had actually saved her from the sex trade. But that was not a story he could tell these good folk. "Suffice it to say, her father had debts."

Mrs. Hopkins folded her hands against her apron. "Ah," she said sagely. "That is not an uncommon fate for girls. Most have no say to their lives."

"And perhaps what happened to Miss Inglewood happened because she tried to have control of her life," James said calmly as he cut open the pastie.

She looked at him, an arrested expression in her eyes. "Yes…perhaps I misspoke to call her a witch."

James shrugged. "She sounds to me like an intelligent, willful, and spoiled young woman who lacked proper guidance."

Mrs. Hopkins sighed. "True." She shook her head, then went around the side of the bar to pick up the empty bowls and plates of others in the pub.

"I've heard you set a man to making repairs at the church," Mr. Hopkins said, leaning on the bar.

Sir James swallowed and took a sip of ale before answering. "Yes."

The innkeeper shook his head. "I would have thought Mortlake would see to repairs."

"If he knew of the need, I'm sure he would," Sir James said, taking another bite of the pastie and washing it down with more ale.

They were veering away from the subjects that interested James the most. He tried another tack.

"Is young Mr. Inglewood like his sister, Georgia?" James asked, curious to know more about the Inglewood family. He and Cecilia had exchanged greetings with the Squire and his family after Sunday church services; however, they did not know the family beyond that time.

Mr. Hopkins shook his head. "Like night and day—in looks and temperament," he said. "A steady young man, for the most part, though his sister rattled him. He stays away from home as much as he can."

Sir James nodded his understanding, but privately

wondered if he stayed away because of his sister or his father. Or both. "I was wondering why he wasn't at the inquest. He must be away now."

"Aye, that he be. In Folkestone, or wherever Captain Horsley be."

"Mortlake's yacht captain?"

Mr. Hopkins nodded. "The same. Young Inglewood is sailing mad, and the captain has been teaching him navigation —with the earl's permission."

James nodded thoughtfully. "Ah, then he is likely on his way back. Mortlake sent the captain to fetch Miss Faith Jones back to Mertonhaugh." Sir James finished the last of his pastie and pushed his platter forward.

"Where might that be from?"

Sir James merely smiled and shook his head.

Mr. Hopkins chuffed good-naturedly. "Another ale?"

James started to say no until a dark shadow blocked the light streaming in the open front door. Every head in the bar turned to see the newcomer. The dark shadow resolved into the figure of Viscount Kendell.

"Lord Kendell!" the innkeeper said heartily.

Kendell crossed the room to the bar to slouch on a stool next to James with all the insouciance common among young men. Mr. Hopkins placed a mug of beer in front of him without the viscount asking. "What has you looking so down, my lord?" he asked.

The viscount huffed, then straightened to pick up his beer, then slouched. "My oh so lovely half-sister arrived yesterday," he said morosely. He wrapped his hand around the beer mug and raised it to his lips, downing half the contents. He wiped his lips with the back of his hand.

"I assume this is the half-sister who's been in London?" James said as he motioned to Mr. Hopkins to pour him another ale. He settled back on his stool.

Kendell nodded. "Hope. Father—and even Mother!—are fawning all over her." He shook his head. "I had to get out of the house."

He straightened slightly and burped. James didn't imagine this was his first beer of the day.

"You said two nights ago you wanted to meet your half-sisters," James reminded him.

He swigged his beer, his lips compressed in a flat line. "I did," he admitted. "…Tell me, Sir James, you're a gentleman of parts, are all females the same? Giggly and squealy," he asked, imitating the sounds, "like Gussie and Marty and Georgia?"

Mr. Hopkins laughed, and the viscount glowered at him. Mr. Hopkins went to the other end of the bar to refill some drinks.

The viscount stared down into his mug. "I need to get out of this God-forsaken village. I wonder if father will finance a grand tour for me," he groused to James.

James frowned. "You say Miss Jones was giggly? I'm surprised given the sad circumstances for her visit."

"She was sad enough when she came, dressed all in black and all, then Father and Mother got to talking with her and discovered she'd recently got some hapless dolt to ask her to marry him."

"And that was when the giggles and squeals began," James concluded. "You don't seem to be much in favor of the wedded state."

"No, I'm not. At least not now; I ain't ready.—And so I told Georgia at least half a dozen times."

"Determined to sow some wild oats first?" James asked laconically.

"It's a man's rite of passage!"

James raised an eyebrow at the viscount, much like he would have done to a junior officer who spewed nonsense.

"Is that what you were doing with Miss Inglewood?"

"What? No—I knew better. Father made sure I knew! Oh, we flirted, yes. She was fun to be around, but no. Nothing else. Nothing. No matter what she said, or anyone else."

"I hadn't known she said elsewise. What did she say?"

"She had it in her beautiful little noggin that I would be an easy catch, and she could be a countess. Said it would be to my advantage to marry her. I never could figure out how she came up with that notion. Woolly-headed female."

"From what I have heard of her, I would have thought she would hold out for a duchess, or at least a marchioness."

"That's what I thought, too, but she up and decided she'd have the baby she carried and tell everyone it was mine unless I got her some pennyroyal. Damned fool chit."

"And did you?" James asked. Out of the corner of his eye, he noted Mr. Hopkins sliding more in their direction, listening.

"What?" Kendell asked, irritated.

"Get her pennyroyal."

Kendell reared backward on his stool. "No! –Well, I couldn't," he admitted, leaning forward again. "The apothecary in Maidstone was out of the herb. Had a run on it recently. Said it only grows in marshy areas, like Romney Marsh, and he likely wouldn't get any more for another month or more." He waved his empty beer mug in the innkeeper's direction. Mr. Hopkins hurried forward to grab his mug and refill it.

"When did this happen? When did you go to Maidstone?"

The viscount's face screwed up as he considered. He scratched the back of his head. "I think two days before she died… Yes. Two days, because that's when I got three new decks of cards from the stationers for game night."

"Game night?" James repeated.

"Once or twice a month at the brewery. Low stakes, as most around here don't have the coin for more. Gives me practice for when I go to London. I intend to win big in London," he said. He grabbed one hand with the other and cracked his knuckles, a schoolboy brag.

"I see," James said slowly. "And when do you intend to take London by storm?"

"In the fall, during the little season. That's when my mother wants to go. I'll go with her and enjoy myself *otherwise*," he said, wriggling his eyebrows. "When I'm not playing the dutiful son escorting her around." He laughed. He slouched on the bar again.

"Lord Kendell, I'd venture you had nought to eat today," said Mrs. Hopkins. She set a bowl of stew before him along with a large chunk of bread. "Eat. Ya need somethin' in your gullet other than beer, though fine Mortlake beer it be. Eat!" She shoved a spoon in his hand and then turned to go back to her kitchen.

"Managing female," Kendell slurred, but he did dip the spoon in the hearty stew for a bite.

Sir James laughed. He looked over at Mr. Hopkins. "Quite like Lady Branstoke." He tossed coins on the bar and slid off his stool. He clasped Kendell's shoulder. "Best take Mrs. Hopkin's advice and eat the stew. You'll need your strength. Remember, Miss Hope Jones has a sister, and she might be here by tomorrow if the tides and weather stay in Captain Horsley's favor."

Kendell slid him a side-eyed glance. "You don't need to spoil my meal."

Sir James merely laughed again and left the tavern to return to Summerworth. It was time to compare notes with his darling wife.

CHAPTER 10

PUZZLE PIECES

"Thank you, Daniel. What you witnessed was much like I expected. Sir James and I are appreciative of your efforts," Cecilia said when Daniel returned from his task.

"I should be happy to assist at any time in your inquiries," the footman said formally with the appropriate amount of reserve Mr. Coggins would approve; however, his eyes gave away his eagerness.

Cecilia laughed. "You have been bitten by the inquiry bug. I'll own it can be invigorating. But dangerous as well," she warned him.

"Have you ever been in danger, my lady?" Daniel asked.

"Several times, much to Sir James' dismay," she answered wryly.

Daniel's eyes widened. "I should imagine so, my lady... Will you be wanting your tea now, or do you wish to wait for Sir James?"

"I'll wait for Sir James," she said. "I can use the time to catch up on the news from London," she told him as she picked up one of the newspapers she'd brought to the sofa.

The cat jumped up on her lap, crushing the newspaper under him. "Well, I will catch up when Randy allows me to," she owned, scratching the cat's head.

∾

AFTER LEAVING the Sheep's Head Tavern, James went to the church to see how Mr. McCurdy was progressing with the repairs to the pulpit. To his initial dismay, the entire platform had been dismantled, with the decorative wood neatly stacked to the side.

"Do you judge this repair task to be completed by Sunday?" he asked his carpenter as he studied the mess of new and old lumber.

"Och, aye, Sir James," Mr. McCurdy said jovially. "The worst is done past. Evrathing's measured and cut. I'll be rebuildin' the platform today and stainin' it tommorra."

"Any other trouble with people coming to gossip about Mrs. Jones?"

"Aye, sar, but that Mrs. Hull, she be a feisty one and beat me to sending them on their way. And she sent them off with a flea in their ear, too."

James laughed, then became serious. "So long as we can ease the vicar's burden and not let others malign Mrs. Jones. One of his daughters has arrived in Mertonhaugh. Has she come to visit the vicar?"

Mr. McCurdy shook his head. "No, sar, and I knows Mrs. Hull is getting' down right irritated at that. I wouldna put it past 'er to march right up to the big house and drag the gel to the vicarage."

"Neither would I. I'll speak with her."

Mr. McCurdy nodded and bent to pick up a new board to fasten to the platform structure. James turned to go to the vicarage.

He discovered Mrs. Hull in the herb garden, talking to the weeds she pulled out. She told them, quite in stern tones, that this garden was not the place for them to be growing. He couldn't help but smile.

"Excuse me, Mrs. Hull," James said gently so as not to frighten the woman.

"Oh! Sir James. You caught me weeding Mrs. Jones' herb garden," she said on straightening.

"And telling the weeds the garden is not a place for them to be growing."

She laughed. "Well, yes," she said brightly, not offering any apology or explanation. She instead winked at James.

"Mr. McCurdy tells me you are not happy with Miss Jones for not visiting her father and staying at the Mortlake Manor."

Her lips compressed. "That be true. What an unnatural child. He raised her, wiped her tears, built a swing on the old oak in the far corner of the church grounds, played games with her and her sister. He was a good father to her and Faith. Then, when they found out their real father is an earl, they abandoned him. I understood when they first found out, that I did. Mrs. Jones and I discussed it. They were angry at her and spread their anger to the vicar when all he ever did was love them like they were his own. But it's been neigh on three years!" the woman said, her ire rising. "I've a mind to go tell them what I think of them."

"I can understand your desire to do so. All I ask is that you don't and let Lady Branstoke and me handle this. I feel we can get them to see the error of their ways."

She looked at him steadily for a moment, frowning, then she reluctantly nodded. "I will, at least until Mrs. Jones be laid to rest."

"That will be time enough, and if they are still angry at the vicar, they shall be deserving of your wrath," James told her. He thanked her for her promise and left the church property. It was teatime and playtime with his young son, something he didn't care to miss.

CECILIA ALLOWED James to relax and dawdle Hugh on his knee before her patience expired. "You went to the brewery this morning."

"Yes," her husband said as he raised his son above his head. Hugh giggled.

"Well, did you learn anything?"

"Yes. The making of beer and ale is quite fascinating. I learned that here in Kent, they don't make beer during the summer, as the weather is too warm for the beer to cool quickly," he told her.

"James!" she admonished. She set her teacup back on the table with a rattle of china.

Hugh spat up, the milky substance landing on James' jacket.

Cecilia quickly grabbed Hugh from James so he might wipe up the mess. "Serves you right for swinging him above your head as you did so soon after he's eaten. Your valet will be irritable."

"No, he won't. He is conversant with the behavior of

babies from his mother's household. He likes them," he said as he casually wiped away the spittle from his jacket.

"Liking is not the same as removing baby stains from clothing," observed Cecilia.

James canted his head a moment, then acknowledged her comment as he looked at the stain on his jacket.

"I believe that was Hugh's way of helping me grab the reins and drive you to the topic we should be discussing. Miss Inglewood, Mrs. Jones, and pennyroyal. –Daniel, ask Mrs. Threadmont to retrieve Master Hugh. He requires a change of clothing."

"At once, my lady," said their attentive footman.

After Hugh had been placed in the devoted care of Mrs. Threadmont, Cecilia refreshed their tea and looked expectantly at her husband.

"Mr. Vernon talked to me directly. He did not glance away or otherwise subtly indicate he was not truth-telling. He did enjoy her company until it became clear to him that her charms were well shared. I believe that caused him to retreat from that relationship, though the young woman continued to send him notes and entreaties."

"I'm sure she didn't believe that any man could be immune to her charms and wiles for long," Cecilia said. "She thought quite highly of herself."

James agreed. "He did say something about Squire Inglewood that was interesting. At one time our magistrate arrested Mr. Vernon as a libertine and threw him into his gaol. He also seems to have spread a rumor that Mr. Vernon suffers from a sexual affliction."

"What!" Cecilia declared. "Why would he do that?"

"I don't know. I can conjecture that he wanted to demean

Mortlake and the Mortlake Brewery. Possibly revenge for Kendell not showing interest in marrying his daughter, even before she claimed she was enceinte."

"He wanted a title for his daughter."

"That is my thought. However, Mortlake and Dr. Patterson visited the magistrate and immediately after, Mr. Vernon was freed and the gossip recanted."

"Interesting," Cecilia said. "I wonder what was said—or threatened—to achieve that."

James shrugged.

"I'm sure our housekeeper will be pleased to know her nephew was not one of Miss Inglewood's crowd."

"Speaking of her crowd, I did learn where the gamekeeper's cottage is from Mr. Vernon."

"Excellent! I'd like to visit it tomorrow," Cecilia said.

"If you are hoping to find any evidence there, her family and her friends most likely searched the cottage after her death," James cautioned.

Cecilia nodded, a wayward curl of her white-blonde hair falling out of her coif. "Yes, but sometimes familiarity with a space reduces thoughts of possibilities."

James agreed as he reached over to push the wayward strand away from her face. She smiled lovingly at him.

He took another sip of tea and set his cup down. "After the brewery, I went to The Sheep's Head Tavern. The owners are an interesting couple. Owning the tavern, they hear about everything going on in town."

"I well believe that."

"I asked them about George Inglewood, Miss Inglewood's brother."

"Isn't he older than Miss Inglewood? Odd that Inglewood would name siblings who were not twins with similar names."

"Squire Inglewood is an odd man. I am of the impression that he is not a loving father. Young George Inglewood is sailing mad and spends most of his time away from home in Folkestone with Captain Horsley, learning all about sailing. He probably went with the captain to fetch Miss Faith Jones. That reminds me, Miss Hope Jones has arrived at Mortlake House, but she has not visited the vicar. And Kendell told me she is engaged to be married, which has him twisted in a knot because that is all she talks of with his parents."

"You were busy collecting bits and pieces," Cecilia said, delighted.

"This is an investigation that requires bits and pieces versus the broad actions we've been accustomed to."

"Like one of Spilbury's map puzzles."

"One for which we're missing pieces," he said with his usual laconic dryness.

Cecilia laughed. "Yes, but we will collect them all, I'm sure of it."

"To that end, I shall have Romley spend more time at the tavern and in town to see if he can catch wind of when young Mr. Inglewood returns."

"I could do that for you, sir!" Daniel offered from the side of the room.

James' brow furrowed as he looked in the direction of the footman.

Cecilia laughed. She laid her hand on her husband's arm. "He did a bit of investigating for me this afternoon and found he quite liked it," she said quietly.

James looked back at Cecilia. "What did he do?"

"Miss Sandiford was here this afternoon to deliver some ells of cloth to me. I invited her to rest and have lemonade. In my conversation about Miss Inglewood—who she seems to idolize—I told her how dangerous pennyroyal is. She did not seem to know that, and the knowledge prompted her to leave. I had Daniel follow her. Ultimately, she met with Miss Broadbank in what appeared to be secrecy."

"It doesn't surprise me that so few knew the dangers of the plant… Daniel, see if you can find this gamekeeper's cottage. I have learned it is close to the southeast corner of the Inglewood property." James looked at Cecilia. "The gamekeeper kept chickens, and they tended to wander into the Inglewood garden. Inglewood complained; consequently, Mortlake built a new cottage for the gamekeeper on the other side of his estate." He looked back up at Daniel. "I doubt it will be directly off the road. Lady Branstoke wants to visit the cottage, so previous knowledge of its location would help."

"Yes, sir, I can do that!" Daniel said brightly.

"You may go now. Be sure to let Mr. Coggins know you are going on an errand for us."

"Thank you, sir. I won't let you down."

James smiled, and Cecilia hid a slight chuckle behind her hand as the young man hurried to leave.

"DANIEL WAS MOST fervent in his desire to do a good job," Cecilia said as she studied the small piece of paper Daniel had given them at breakfast that morning. "He's drawn a detailed map to the old cottage."

"I commend his enthusiasm and effort," James said.

"Will you allow him to assist in the future?" Cecilia asked, canting her head.

"Possibly; however, I am concerned he hasn't the maturity for caution."

Cecilia acknowledged his concern. "Still, if we are going to continue to be involved in inquiries, it would be beneficial to have others we may direct, much like Mr. Thornbridge was an asset."

"He appears to be an even greater asset for my cousin, judging from the letters I've received," James said.

"That is good to know. I'm happy for him."

"Even if you couldn't match him with Miss Rangaswamy?" James asked slyly.

Cecilia sighed. "Yes, but I'll own the Earl of Soothcoor's half-brother has been a surprisingly successful match."

"Why do you say 'surprisingly'? He matches her in liveliness."

"True," she conceded. "And she has steadied him in other ways."

"Mr. Thornbridge will find his way," James said, "just as we are finding ours to this gamekeeper's cottage. According to Daniel's map, after that big oak up ahead, there will be a faint trail to the left that we follow."

"I'm glad I chose to wear one of my older dresses. This wood is thick with vegetation. I'll likely acquire burrs and seed pods on my hem," she observed as they turned onto the path Daniel had drawn on the map. The trees were thick and nearly hid the sky. Cecilia closed her parasol. She did not need it in the shade wrought by the surrounding trees.

Together, they walked for another ten minutes before a stone cottage came into view. Without trees above, sunlight streamed down on the little cottage, burnishing its stones to a warm hue. Vines climbed the chimney and extended along the bottom edge of the roof, rooting under slate tiles green with moss and mildew. One of the glass windowpanes on the front of the building was broken, and it looked like someone had fastened a piece of leather at the opening to keep the elements out. The cottage had been built on an elevated area of land, and large, flat stones formed steps up to the front door.

"It looks in fairly good condition for being abandoned. I wonder how long ago the new gamekeeper's cottage was built?" Cecilia said.

"This cottage appears snug and exceedingly well built," James said. "A pity it was abandoned." He pressed on the door latch. It was unlocked. He glanced at Cecilia, his brows raised in surprise.

"If this was their club, it stands to reason it would be unlocked," Cecilia said as James pushed the door open.

The one-room cottage showed signs that the young women had tried to make the space more comfortable. Mismatched drapes, probably retrieved from the Inglewood attic, hung at the windows. A vase with dead flowers sat on the table pushed against the back wall under a window. Wood chairs had small pillows on their seats. A threadbare rug of Persian design covered the rough wood floor. And on the wall opposite, an old, narrow bed had been enlivened with a colorful quilt and several mismatched pillows. A kettle hung from a hook over the fireplace. The cottage smelled of wood smoke and damp mold.

Cecilia crossed the room to the fireplace. She ran a gloved finger across the mantelpiece. "It is relatively clean," she said, looking at her glove. "But I don't feel anyone has come here since Miss Inglewood passed." She pulled the armoire door open. A lone woman's cloak hung on a peg.

"Are you looking for something in particular?" James asked as Cecilia pulled open the drawers at the base of the armoire.

"Yes. Miss Inglewood's journal. Summer said she kept it here. Since it doesn't look like anyone has been here in a while, it might still be here."

"At least not since immediately after her death," James acknowledged. "While you look around here, I'll find the old hen house and see if any missives remain in that location, and if there are, what they might tell us."

Cecilia vaguely nodded, her eyes roaming the room, her mind considering where a journal might be hidden. After poking in all the drawers and boxes, she approached the bed. She stood with her hands on her hips as she considered the narrow bed. She leaned over to pull up one corner of the mattress to see if the journal might be hidden beneath the bedding.

The light from the open cottage door sliced further under the bed when she picked up the bedding. Her heart raced, and her smile grew broad. "Found you," she whispered gleefully, for through the knotted rope net that supported the mattress, she saw the edge of an open book stuck between the wall and the bedstead.

Cecilia started to pull the bed away from the wall when she heard voices outside. She turned to look out the door. James and two young men—who looked amazingly alike— approached the cottage. The Cathcart twins, she surmised. They were, indeed, strapping young men with curly blond hair. As they got closer, Cecilia could see they were strikingly handsome, though younger than they had first appeared. She doubted they had yet reached their majority. She could see why Summer's eyes sparkled when she talked of them—and why Miss Inglewood would play them off each other.

And she wondered why they were here. She stepped into the doorway to greet them.

"James, I know you went to the hen house to see what you could find in it. I find it hard to believe you found these gentlemen there. How did they fit?" she teased.

The two young men looked confused, but her husband laughed. "There wasn't much to find. It is too small. I'm not surprised that only Miss Inglewood and Miss Rutledge used the structure. It is too small for even a decent hen house.

"My dear, allow me to make you known to Mr. Jebus and Mr. Josiah Cathcart—but don't ask me which is which, for I'm afraid I don't know. Gentlemen, this is my wife, Lady Branstoke."

After one twin backhanded the other in his stomach, the twins bowed quickly.

"Pleased to meet you, my lady," said the one who had backhanded the other. "I am Josiah, and this be Jebus."

"The blacksmith's sons," Cecilia said for her own clarification.

"Yes, my lady," bobbed Josiah.

"These gentlemen tell me they came here to see if they could find Miss Inglewood's diary," James told her with a pronounced drawl.

Cecilia raised her chin as she looked from one twin to the other. "Miss Inglewood has been deceased for a fortnight now. Why the sudden interest in her diary?"

Cecilia watched, fascinated, as blushes rose from their

necks to suffuse their faces. James crossed his arms over his chest and leaned against the doorframe, listening with a slight smirk on his lips, one only Cecilia could recognize for what it was.

"We was chopping wood this morning, sayin' as how it sure were sad that Miss Inglewood were gone."

"Yes," Jebus agreed, speaking for the first time while nodding vigorously.

"And Jebus remembered her scribbling away in her book. He wondered what she said about us."

Jebus nodded.

"I said no one has said nothin' about her book. I wondered if anyone had found it. Jebus said we should look for it."

"Well, Jebus seems to have a great many ideas," Cecilia said.

Josiah Cathcart nodded. "Very thoughtful is my brother, Jebus."

Cecilia looked at Jebus. "Where would you suggest we look for the book?"

He pointed to the floor inside the cottage. Cecilia and James exchanged glances. Cecilia always knew James' thoughts when they did so.

"Please come in and show us. Our thought is the book may give us clues as to why she died when she did."

Jebus, followed by Josiah, came into the cabin. Without speaking, they went to either end of the rug on the floor and rolled it back. They carefully pulled up a board.

"I thought there might be a loose board, but I didn't consider it would be so far under the rug," Cecilia said quietly to James as they stepped closer to see what the twins did.

Jebus reached into the hole and pulled out a light-brown leather bag tied with what looked to be a drapery cord. He frowned as he shook it. He looked at his brother. "It's not here," he said, the most words Cecilia or James had yet heard him speak.

"May I?" Cecilia asked, reaching out for the bag. Jebus handed it to her, then reached down into the hole again. Cecilia saw him frown and sit back on his heels when he pulled out his hand, not finding anything else in the hiding place.

The bag was fairly light and soft. It crinkled when squeezed, releasing the scent of a kind of odd mint. She wrinkled her nose. It was not a scent she favored.

She loosened what looked like an old gold drapery cord holding it closed and opened it. Her brow lifted slightly at the sight of the contents. She passed it to James to look inside. She didn't know for certain; however, she'd wager the bag held enough pennyroyal for a grand, murderous tea party. A shiver went down Cecilia's spine.

Josiah stood up and looked in the bag. "Is that the stuff she wanted?"

"I believe so," Cecilia said.

"Huh." Josiah turned to look at his brother. "It's no wonder that apothecary said he were runnin' low and could only give us a small amount."

"Which apothecary was that?" James asked.

"Thorne's in Maidstone."

"You and your brother tried to buy pennyroyal for Miss Inglewood?" James continued.

"Yeah. She begged us, ya see. But he didn't have much left. We took what he had," Josiah said as Jebus rose to his feet to stand beside him.

"Sold out," Jebus added.

"Did either of you ask who else had purchased the plant?"

"Yes, sar," Jebus said, surprising Cecilia. "He wouldn't say."

"As would be proper," James said, nodding. "An ethical apothecary."

Cecilia nodded. "Ethical, but disappointing for our purposes."

James looked at Cecilia. "We may need to go to Maidstone," he said solemnly.

"Have you any other ideas where Miss Inglewood may have hidden the book?" Cecilia asked. "I have looked in all other places I could think of, including under the bed linens and under the bed." For some reason, she couldn't answer for herself, Cecilia did not want to reveal to the twins that she may have found the book. She wanted James and her to review the book first before others. She had a feeling that what Miss Inglewood wrote would not be complimentary to most of her associates.

"We'd best get back," Josiah said to Jebus. "Pa will be lookin' fer us."

Jebus nodded.

"Sorry we didn't find the book," Josiah said to Cecilia and James.

"That is quite all right," Cecilia told him. "You did lead us to something that is perhaps more interesting."

They both nodded, then left.

Cecilia watched them walk down the path away from the cottage, then she shut the door.

"I presume you do know where the diary is?" James said to Cecilia. She smiled up at him.

"Help me move the bed away from the wall."

As they pulled the bed away, they heard a thunk. Cecilia

ran around to the back of the bed. "When I picked up the mattress to look under it, I thought I saw a book caught between the bed and the wall." She bent over to reach down between the wall and the bed and pulled out a book.

She started to eagerly open it. James placed his hand over hers. "Not here," he said. "I do not trust that others will not come." He took the book from her and tucked it in his jacket pocket. "Let's return home."

CHAPTER 11

GEORGE INGLEWOOD

There was a loud commotion coming out of the Sheep's Head Tavern when Cecilia and James came upon it on their way home. In their typical communication style, with merely a glance at each other, they agreed to enter the tavern to see what was going on.

It was George Inglewood standing in a circle of men from the village, toasting his return with cheers and echoes of "Congratulations!" He was grinning and clinking mugs with each man in turn. From what they could hear, the Branstokes concluded George had bought a round for all the people in the tavern.

James and Cecilia approached George as the crowd around George began to disperse. "Did you go with Captain Horsley to Devon?" James asked.

"That I did," George said gleefully, "and the Captain let *me* take charge of the yacht on our return! I've been unofficially apprenticing under him for almost a year now, and this is the first time he's let me captain the yacht. He said I'm a natural!

I'm chuffed. I haven't been able to stop grinning since we docked."

"Let us add to the congratulations," Cecilia enthused. "That does call for a toast." She turned toward the bar. "Mr. Hopkins, an ale for my husband and me, please… Shall we sit?" Cecilia suggested when Mr. Hopkins slid the drinks over the bar to her. "I should like to hear about your trip."

"Yes! Of course." George followed James and Cecilia to a table in a corner away from the others in the tavern.

"Did you bring Miss Faith Jones back with you?" James asked.

"Yes. I left her at Mortlake Manor. She was an odd sort, didn't know if she wanted to cry or be angry."

"I can understand that," Cecilia said. "The vicar said she wrote a letter to her mother to explain her anger and perhaps mend their relationship."

"That was my understanding, and she was angry she didn't have a chance to do that. But I didn't get a chance to speak with her much, as I was sailing us back to Folkestone as swiftly as the winds would let us come."

"You made good time," James observed.

"Yes, we did. Captain Horsley told me the earl wanted us to make haste. Oh—the Duke of Monteith handed me a letter to give to you on our return here. Unfortunately, I put it in my portmanteau which I sent on home."

"I'll get it from you later," James told him. "Thank you for bringing it."

"That duke wasn't happy about Miss Jones leaving with us. Said it was a bad time. She told him she would stay if he felt strongly about it. He got rather angry then, and told her she had to go."

"Interesting," James said, now curious about the letter George had. His cousin was not known for having a temper. Had he a tendre for Miss Jones?

A lovely smell came from the direction of the kitchen. "Ummm. I smell something enticing," Cecilia said.

"Mrs. Hopkins' pasties," James told her.

"Are you hungry, Mr. Inglewood? My husband told me Mrs. Hopkins makes delicious pasties, and I am rather famished," Cecilia said.

"I've been too chuffed to eat."

"Well, you should eat. I'll ask Hopkins if we might have three pasties," Cecilia said, rising from the table.

James watched his wife walk away, then turned back to face George. "I've been wanting to talk to you about your sister's death. And the death of Mrs. Jones."

"I heard about Mrs. Jones' death," he said. "I've been away from Mertonhaugh since two days after my sister's death."

"Your father wants to declare Mrs. Jones' death a suicide. He believes she suffered guilt for your sister's death and therefore ended her own life."

George barked out a sharp laugh. "Not likely! My father likes to have truth match his *created* narrative. He has always been like that. Truth is not the truth unless it matches what he believes should be the truth," he said bitterly.

"Why does he want Mrs. Jones' death classified as suicide other than to see that she is buried in an unconsecrated grave?"

"Because she was one of the people who did not automatically agree with everything he said, nor did she do as he wished. To my mind, the worst thing that ever happened to my father was being named magistrate for the area. He asked for it, you know, and no one ran against him."

"No, I didn't know," James said.

"No, I guess you wouldn't," George said remorsefully. He waved at Mr. Hopkins for another beer. "It was before you moved here."

Cecilia came back to the table. "Mrs. Hopkins put a fresh batch of pasties in the oven. She'll bring them over when they're done."

"You had an opportunity to meet Mrs. Hopkins, then?" James asked.

"Yes!" Cecilia said, grinning. "And she said she could arrange for someone else to help Mr. Hopkins so she could come to tea—after I convinced her she was welcome in our home. I'll invite Elinor, too."

"Good," James said.

"Have you asked Mr. Inglewood about his sister yet?"

"No, we have been discussing Mrs. Jones and why his father wishes her death could be named a suicide."

"What is it you want to know about my sister?" Mr. Inglewood asked.

"We know that she asked several people in the village to get her pennyroyal. Did she ask you as well?"

"Yes. I wasn't going to get it for her. I saw no need for she had already received packets from several people. I told her that, too. Father insisted I get her more pennyroyal and told me to visit the apothecary in Folkestone to see if he had any. Worse luck, he did, and I gave it to my father."

"Not to your sister directly?" Cecilia asked sharply.

He shook his head. "Father said to give it to him when I returned, and he'd see it was added to her canister. I asked him why she felt she had to have so much. He shrugged and said that was my sister's way."

George accepted another mug of beer from Mr. Hopkins. "I loved my sister, I did, but she was a hard person to love. She thought a great deal of herself, like she were the daughter of a king, not a squire. Everyone was to do as she asked. She and Father were much alike."

"And that is probably why they did not get along," Cecilia offered.

He nodded. "She was always trying to make him dance to her tune. That could be amusing at times and at others, depressing. Mother and I were spectators of their conflict."

Mrs. Hopkins brought their pasties out to them, steam rising from the vents. Cecilia inhaled the aroma. "Smells heavenly, Mrs. Hopkins," she said.

Mrs. Hopkins smiled. "Thank you, my lady. Would you like more ale?"

"I'll take another ale," James said.

"Do you have any lemonade?" Cecilia asked.

"I do. I keep some fresh for the ladies, should they come in."

Cecilia winked at her. "Good idea. I'll have some, please."

"Right away, my lady."

"What did your mother think about what your sister did?" James asked Mr. Inglewood when Mrs. Hopkins went to fetch their beer and lemonade.

"She was horrified! However, Father said to let her be. He had plans for her that he saw her stepping right into, like leading a horse to water. If Georgia had known that, she would have been enraged."

"Did they always work at cross purposes to each other?" James asked.

"Always," Mr. Inglewood said on a heavy sigh.

The three of them ate in silence for a moment.

"You know, my sister took sick in that gamekeeper's cottage she liked," George suddenly said.

"I was wondering," Cecilia said quietly.

He nodded his head.

"What state was she in?" James asked.

"Mrs. Hester came and got me. By the time I got to the cottage, Georgia said her belly hurt so fiercely she couldn't walk. I carried her back to the house," he said, memories firing across his face, "her losing her stomach on herself—and me. I got her up to her room, then Mother and Father came up and Father told me to go clean myself up and get out of the house. I came here," he admitted, looking around at the familiar insides of the Sheep's Head.

"How long did you stay here?" James asked.

"At least four hours. I didn't leave until a servant came to tell me my sister had died. I knew our father was behind it," he said bitterly. "I knew Georgia didn't want to die or even take any pennyroyal concoction. I suspected by her manner that she had already lost the child she carried. He wanted her dead."

Cecilia gasped, this wasn't something she had considered; however, it made a twisted form of sense. "Why would he want his own daughter's death?"

"Because he couldn't control her," George said sadly.

"Does he control you?" Cecilia asked gently.

"He thinks he does, but I don't throw my rebellious feelings in his face."

"You do things like quietly learn to be a ship's captain."

He looked at her. "Yes. I tried to tell Georgia that she would do better being subtle, but there wasn't a subtle bone in Georgia's body."

"No, I can see that," Cecilia said sadly.

"Pardon, Sir James," said their footman, Daniel, coming up to them in the tavern. He held out a cream-colored invitation. "Mr. Coggins felt this might be important and asked me to seek you out," he said.

Cecilia took the invitation from him, her expression skewed into confusion. She slid a fingernail under the lightly sealed envelope. She pulled out a handwritten note to join the Mortlakes for dinner that night to welcome home both of the Jones daughters.

"Well," said Cecilia as she handed the card to James, "I hope the vicar is invited."

"I do as well," he stated after reading the card. "Please excuse us, Mr. Inglewood. We need to return to our home to prepare for another engagement this evening. And allow me to say once again, congratulations with your success in your sailing."

"Thank you, Sir James," said Inglewood, not looking up at them, his sad attention fixed upon his beer.

"Do you suppose he'll be all right?" Cecilia asked James softly as they left the tavern. "He'd been in such high spirits, and I'm afraid we dashed him to the ground. I hate to leave him like that."

"I agree; however, I also deem it is time he acknowledges to himself—really acknowledges—what his father has done."

"What do you mean?"

"He said his father wanted her dead, but I don't feel he has accepted that belief in his heart, in his soul."

"He may not have; however, I do. His father, *our* magistrate, deliberately killed his daughter, Georgia Inglewood."

Cecilia tucked her arm through her husband's and leaned her head against his shoulder. "But there is no proof."

"No, and it doesn't bring us any closer to knowing what happened to Mrs. Jones."

COGGINS MET James and Cecilia at the door to Summerworth Park. "You have visitors, my lady," Coggins intoned formally.

Cecilia cocked her head. "Who?" she asked as they entered.

"A Miss Broadbank and a Miss Sandiford. I have taken the liberty of escorting them to the morning room and supplying them with lemonade and biscuits as I knew with the invitation from the Mortlakes, you would be returning shortly."

"Thank you, Mr. Coggins," Cecilia said. She turned to James. "I wonder what these young women want?"

"Most likely something about Miss Inglewood."

"Yes, I'd best not keep them waiting lest they become doubtful of their errand and seek to leave. Do you wish to join me?"

"No, I'm sure the young ladies will talk more freely with you if I am not around. I'll go upstairs to tell my valet and your maid we shall be going out tonight so they may take out and press appropriate attire."

She nodded to him and turned to the morning room.

She paused at the doorway for a moment, looking at her guests. They looked the picture of misery. That wouldn't do.

"Hello, my dears! To what do I owe the pleasure of your visit?" she asked walking briskly into the room. The young women sat side by side on the sofa, holding each other's hands. They stood up quickly. Cecilia saw their eyes were puffy and red when they looked at her. She recognized one of the young women as Augusta Sandiford.

"Excuse us for presumption," said Augusta. "But we really need to talk to you."

"I am happy to talk to you. I find, however, that I do not know your companion…"

"Oh! Yes, I'm sorry," Augusta said, red sweeping up her neck. "This is my friend Martha Broadbank."

Cecilia smiled at Martha. "I have heard your name before. It's nice to meet you. Now, let's sit, and please have a biscuit and lemonade. Cook makes a delicious lemonade."

She sat in an armchair at a right angle to them.

"So, tell me, what is the matter? What has you all in a dither?" she asked gently.

"Oh, Lady Branstoke, we killed her!" Augusta said, her voice breaking as she forced the words out.

"We didn't know!" wailed Martha.

"Didn't know what?" Cecilia asked.

Martha sniffed, followed by a shuddering breath. "We—we didn't know pennyroyal was poisonous."

Augusta nodded. She swiped a wadded and damp handkerchief across her nose. "Until you told me pennyroyal was dangerous, that it could easily kill if not handled properly, we just—just thought it was a tea that could get rid of an unwanted child."

"Oh, I see. You'd never heard Mrs. Jones say anything against it?"

"She did. She stopped us after Sunday service and warned us."

"But you did not believe her."

Martha dropped her head to the side, scrunching her nose as she did so. "No," she said softly, as if she were afraid to speak.

"Why not?" Cecilia asked.

"Because Georgia said not to," Martha admitted in a smaller voice.

Cecilia sighed. "You didn't assume it was the tea that killed her?"

Augusta shook her head. "The coroner and even her father —and he's the magistrate—said it was iliac passion."

"Why don't you believe *now* that she died of iliac passion?"

"Because Mrs. Jones is dead," Augusta said meekly.

Cecilia looked at them silently as she chewed on the biscuit Cook had provided with the lemonade. It amazed her how completely Georgia had had them under her power. She couldn't have been all that manipulative and sarcastic to her friends to have earned the loyalty she saw in these young women.

"You'll have to explain your thinking to me, but we—Sir James and I—believe you are correct in thinking she died from pennyroyal, but you cannot believe you are responsible. Miss Inglewood asked many people to procure pennyroyal for her, and most did. Besides yourselves, we know Mrs. Hester, her brother George, the Cathcart twins, and Mr. Vernon purchased pennyroyal for her. And there may have been others we do not know about. We've been told the apothecary in Maidstone is sold out of the plant."

Augusta's eyes grew round. "It was not cheap."

Cecilia nodded. "No, I don't suppose it was," she said patiently. "Why do you suppose Miss Inglewood asked so many people to purchase pennyroyal for her?"

Martha shrugged, one corner of her lip lifting as she did so. "Because she could?" she suggested.

Augusta nodded, a frown now creasing her brow. "She would want to see who did and who didn't."

"Why would that be important?"

The young women looked at each other. Martha turned back to look at Cecilia. "Maybe to see who she could trust?" she suggested tentatively.

"Or perhaps, who she could control?" Cecilia suggested in return.

Martha frowned, her voice edged. "Are you saying she controlled us?"

"Well, didn't she? And didn't she do the same with Summer and the Cathcart twins, and try to do so with Mr. Vernon and the viscount?"

"She did want everything just so," Augusta admitted.

"Don't you really mean she wanted everything her way?" Cecilia asked.

The young ladies squirmed in their seats. Cecilia decided she'd made her point and given them much to think about.

"Now, what does concern my husband and me is who killed Miss Inglewood. We doubt she would have taken any of that pennyroyal to drink. From everything we have learned, she was not the kind to take her own life."

"No, my lady, that she weren't," affirmed Matha, "and that has had us concerned and confused since the day she died."

"She did say her father kept urging her to drink the tea to purge the babe and get this over with." Augusta shuddered. "I can't imagine doing that; never could. Anyway, Georgia wouldn't listen to him, said there was no need, that she was going to get the Viscount to marry her. She even told him that her father would help her!"

Cecilia's eyebrows rose. "I assume the viscount did not take kindly to that assurance."

"No, but her father was worse!" Martha said, rolling her eyes.

"I don't understand," Cecilia said.

"After we saw and heard the viscount's refusal, we walked with her back to the Inglewood house. We met the squire on the steps. Georgia was still irritated with the viscount so she told her father to pressure the viscount to wed her," Martha explained.

"More like she ordered him," Augusta corrected, "and no, he didn't like that. If we hadn't been there, he might have cuffed her."

Cecilia stroked the side of her cheek with one finger, her brow furrowing as she thought. "I wondered if that wasn't the magistrate's way," she said, more to herself than to the young women.

"We've seen evidence in the past, haven't we, Martha?" Augusta said.

Martha Broadbank nodded sadly.

Cecilia looked between the two women. Thoughts rushed through her mind. If the magistrate was abusive...

"But Georgia, she never backed down," Augusta finished.

"Were you aware she wrote in a diary?" Cecilia asked, wondering how deeply the young women were in Georgia's secrets.

"Yes, she actually kept two diaries, one in her bedroom and one in the cottage."

"Two! Why two?" Cecilia asked. That there were two diaries was not something she had expected.

"She liked writing in a diary, but one day, Mrs. Hester spied her father in her bedroom reading her diary. She told Georgia. Georgia had always been afraid he might, so she hadn't written about him hitting her or anything like that. The diary she kept in the cottage was her real diary, and she said she could allow herself to say anything she wanted in that diary."

"Why keep writing in the diary she kept in her bedroom?"

"To keep him appeased, and, I think, because it amused her to know he was being fooled," Augusta said.

Clever, Cecilia thought. "Have you read her diary? Either of them?"

They shook their heads. "No, we haven't. We went to the cottage after she died to get the diary, but it wasn't in her hiding place," Augusta said.

If the Cathcart twins and these young women both knew of the hiding place, it wasn't a hiding place. Still, she had to be certain that what the twins knew as a hiding place and what the women knew as a hiding place were the same.

"Where was her hiding place?" she asked.

"There was a loose board under the rug she put down. She kept it in there. I do worry where it might be now, and if the magistrate has it."

It was the same place. That appeased Cecilia's mind, but to the young women, Cecilia merely shook her head. "I don't guess he has it, nor even knows about a second diary. I believe his actions, once he discovered it, would have given him away. He is a man who thinks he is inscrutable. He isn't."

"We thought she might have burned the diary," Martha confessed.

"Or maybe Mrs. Jones had it," suggested Augusta.

"Why might you consider Mrs. Jones would have had it?"

"She was angry that Georgia died. She asked us all a lot of questions, same as you."

Cecilia blinked, her gaze sliding past her guests. *Was Mrs. Jones investigating Georgia's death? Could that be why she was killed?*

Cecilia could not tell them she had Georgia's diary, so she only nodded. A nod could mean so many different things. "You've given me a lot to think about," Cecilia told the young women. "I'm glad you came to me. I hope I have given you some comfort in the knowledge you are not responsible for the death of Georgia Inglewood."

"Yes, my lady," Augusta said, rising to her feet. Martha hurried to follow her.

Cecilia saw the two women to the door, then turned to find James coming down the stairs.

"I believe you are right about the magistrate," Cecilia said. "From what Miss Sandiford and Miss Broadbank told me, it appears Mrs. Jones was investigating Georgia Inglewood's death. That could have been the reason for Inglewood's rabid declaration that she killed Miss Inglewood."

James nodded. "But did he kill or frighten Mrs. Jones to her death?" he pondered.

Cecilia sighed. "We still have more investigating to do."

"But at the moment, it is time for Hugh," her husband said, taking her arm to lead her back up the stairs.

Cecilia smiled happily. "Priorities. I do like the way you think, my dear."

CHAPTER 12

A DINNER PARTY

Again, they had Romley drive them to the Mortlakes' estate, and again requested he continue his questioning of the servants, as he might. Romley could be a personable and well-liked person when he chose to be. They felt certain he would be invited into the servants' hall in the manor.

When they arrived at the Mortlakes', they were surprised to find the invitation list small. Besides the Mortlakes, their son, and the twin girls, only the Aldriches, themselves, and the Vicar had been invited. When Cecilia looked questioningly at Lady Elinor Aldrich, already seated in the drawing room, her friend subtly raised her brows at their surprise at the invitation.

The Aldriches had previously been ostracized for Elinor's trade origins. Cecilia wondered if this was a good outcome of gossip created from the story of her first marriage to a merchant. Had the gossip given cause for a widening of the acceptable members of society? Cecilia hoped so. Lord and Lady Aldrich were delightful assets to the community.

"Thank you all for coming," the earl said when the guests had gathered in the drawing room at Mortlake House, a formal room gleaming with gold trim and filled with stiff, upright furniture pieces. It was a room to intimidate others. An interesting choice for this gathering.

Lady Mortlake wore was wearing a charcoal-gray gown, which served to highlight her fading golden hair. On either side of her sat two women who Cecilia surmised were Mrs. Jones' daughters. One wore a fashionable black gown of black bombazine, the other a plain indigo-blue muslin gown with black trim. The women were identical in appearance if one discounted the expressions each wore and their attire.

"Thank you for coming, Lady Branstoke," the countess said, rising to greet her. The women who sat on either side of her rose as well. "Allow me to make you known to Mrs. Jones' daughters, Hope and Faith Jones," she said, indicating the black-attired woman as Hope and the blue-attired woman as Faith. The young women curtsied.

"I'm pleased to meet you," Cecilia said. "I know your relationship with your mother was not the best, but allow me to tell you, I knew her as a good woman, an asset to our community."

"We know," said Hope stiffly. "Yes, I was disappointed in her; however, I loved her always."

"As did I," said Faith.

"I am gratified to hear that," Cecilia said with a warm smile.

"Please sit here," said Lady Mortlake. "I need to circulate more with my guests."

Cecilia nodded and took her seat between the young women.

"My fiancé has spoken of you and your husband," Hope said enthusiastically. "I am delighted to meet you."

"He has? In what context? Who is your fiancé? I must know him," Cecilia said, surprised at this opening to friendship with the sisters.

"He's a solicitor, Richard Hargate of Hargate, Owen, and Hargate."

"Oh, gracious! You are engaged to Richard Hargate! Yes, I do know him. He works almost exclusively for our good friend, the Earl of Soothcoor."

"Who you saved from the hangman's noose last year!" Hope bounced a little on the sofa.

Cecilia noted Faith turning to look at her sister, her interest piquing at their conversation.

Cecilia shrugged. "We had to! Anyone who knows the earl knows he could not have murdered Mr. Montgomery. It was an aberration of justice to even suspect him of murder."

"And before that," Hope went on, "you saved his nephew from life as a chimney sweep."

"My gracious, Mr. Hargate has been telling tales," Cecilia said, smiling at her. She turned to Faith, for she did not wish to be telling tales of the past, and wanted to include her in the conversation. "Did you know my husband is your employer's cousin?" Cecilia asked her.

"He told me when I was leaving. He said if I needed anything, to go to him."

Cecilia smiled. "Yes, and don't hesitate."

"The earl told us that it was Sir Branstoke who spotted our mother after she fell."

Cecilia's smile dimmed. "Yes, he did. And he climbed down the cliff to check on her."

"And she was alive?"

"Yes…but not for long. I sent some water down to my husband, and he was able to wet her mouth so she could speak. He stayed with her until the magistrate and others arrived. We hope he gave her a modicum of comfort before she passed."

"She spoke?" Faith asked, her eyes wide. "What did she say?"

"'No pennyroyal. Stop.' We don't know what her intention was with those words. Miss Georgia Inglewood had passed away some days before your mother, and she had come to Mrs. Jones to ask for pennyroyal. She had turned her down."

"Did she die from pennyroyal?"

"The official cause of death is recorded as iliac passion, a problem with her appendix."

"The recorded cause," said Hope.

"Yes," Cecilia said. "I can tell by that clarifying statement you have spent considerable time around a man who practices law."

Faith raised her hand to mask a laugh at her sister's expense.

Hope bristled, then relaxed and smiled. "Where was the vicar when all this was happening?"

"Your *father*," Cecilia gently corrected, "was told by the magistrate he could not come with them when they went up the downs to where she was."

"Where was he the night before?"

"He'd gone to Canterbury to petition the Archbishop for a curate for the parish. He'd returned home and found she wasn't home. He wasn't immediately concerned, for she had a habit of going up into the downs by herself."

"Really? Our mother go up into the downs? Why?" Faith asked.

"She'd taken up painting," Elinor said, joining them. "She loved painting nature at all times of the day and in all seasons."

"Our mother? Painting?" Hope exclaimed.

"Yes. It was something that she enjoyed." Elinor continued. "She once told me she found it soothing after all the parish demands. She loved the parish and loved what she did for everyone; however, she recognized within herself a need for alone time."

"Cecilia," James said softly, coming up behind her. He gently grasped her elbow.

Cecilia excused herself and stepped away, letting Elinor continue to lead the discussion regarding Mrs. Jones and her role in the community.

James led her over by the fireplace. "Mortlake has asked if we might host the post-burial gathering," he said, his voice low.

Cecilia frowned. "Us? Why?"

"Because we are the closest property of importance to the cemetery, and it would be neutral ground for all."

"Neutral ground? Interesting turn of phrase," she said, contemplating both the rationale and the work involved.

"Only we and the Aldriches are not involved—in any way —with the events that led up to Mrs. Jones' death."

"Meaning Georgia Inglewood's death."

"If we discover who killed Miss Inglewood and why, we discover who killed Mrs. Jones."

"You believe that?" Cecilia asked.

"I do."

Cecilia nodded. "I'll set Mrs. Vernon to preparing for a gathering of the parish. Do we know yet when the funeral will take place?"

"The day after tomorrow."

"Almost a full week since her death."

"But at least before Sunday."

"I hope we are not putting too much confidence in Miss Inglewood's diary for the truth."

"Not too much. We've learned enough about Miss Inglewood to understand she would have needed to brag in some way, and in what better place than her diary?"

"True. –Oh, look, James. The vicar is sitting alone over there. I don't like how the girls have ignored him. Since Lady Mortlake uses dinner place cards, I'm going to ensure they cannot ignore him."

"Don't get caught," James admonished.

She raised her brows at him. "Me? –Go speak to the vicar while I do a bit of table arranging."

CHAPTER 13

THE DIARY OF MISS GEORGIA INGLEWOOD

At breakfast the next morning, James brought with him the diary of Georgia Inglewood. He'd dropped it into his pocket when they left the gamekeeper's cottage the day before. He laid it on the table between himself and Cecilia.

"Have you peeked into it yet?" Cecilia asked.

"No. Truthfully, I find myself loath to do so after all we have learned of this young woman."

"Not a pleasant person," Cecilia suggested. "And yet she had a circle of friends that deferred to her."

"More than deferred, idolized," James said.

"Hmmm, yes. But she must have had some redeeming traits or these young people wouldn't have liked her so. Let's finish breakfast before we delve into it. Best to relax with coffee in the library while we go through the book. I don't know what I wish to find, or where it might lead us."

"Were you happy how events turned out last evening?"

"Yes! You and Lord Aldrich played your roles admirably."

"For all the quick whispered instructions we received before we walked into dinner, telling us to ask the woman we were seated next to about their early life at the vicarage before they went away to school. They were forced to speak of the vicar and all the good memories they had of him as a father. And with him in the middle between them he could chime in on the memories. He certainly got them smiling and laughing."

Cecilia chewed thoughtfully on the last of her toast. "And though Lady Mortlake disapproved of what I did, she was not too upset with me in the end."

"The test will be to see if she invites you to any future dinner parties," James drawled.

Cecilia laughed as she agreed.

THEY SETTLED IN THE LIBRARY, at a round table set before the windows, looking out the south side of the house toward the stables. Outside, Romley was directing a new stable lad on how to cool down James' favorite horse after Romley had exercised him. Romley might be a tough old army campaigner; however, Cecilia always marveled at how patient he could be when teaching others.

She took a sip of her coffee, then pulled the diary toward her, at first flipping through the early pages, full of gossip and sly remarks about her conquests, and the clandestine rendezvous in the cottage. Her quick reading slowed when dates moved closer to Miss Inglewood's death.

"Ah, James. Here is an entry with the same story young

Summer told me about Georgia and the Cathcart twins. Listen:

> *April 23rd*
>
> *I met the Cathcart twins outside the cottage this afternoon. Summer had been telling me something—I don't remember what —when I saw the boys arguing. They were going on about who I smiled at first last Sunday. I don't remember. They look identical to me. Within moments, they were at it, fists flying, shirts flung aside like boys at a fair.*
>
> *I snorted. Highly unladylike, I know, but heavens, what a sight. Their arms glistened with sweat and dirt, and the sun caught every muscle when they swung. Gloriously well-defined blacksmith's muscles. Summer gasped like a child at a puppet show and begged them to stop. I told her to hush—one doesn't interrupt a performance. I—*

"Gracious," Cecilia paused. "The young woman was wanton!" She raised a hand to her fichu and continued reading, her voice higher.

> *I'll own I felt a tingling in my nether region that neither one of them had ever given me before—alone or together.*

James barked a laugh.

"You see what I mean?" Cecilia asked, her eyes wide. She breathed in deeply, then returned to the book.

> *It was glorious while it lasted: two great oafs battering each other for a smile. La! They are as stupid as posts, both of them, but handsome in the rough way of horses.*

"Horses! James, she characterized those nice young gentlemen we met like they are horses. Absolutely disgusting." Cecilia shook her head and continued reading.

When they'd finished, panting and bleeding, they turned to me as if awaiting a prize. I gave each a handkerchief and told them they were both my champions—my blacksmith knights. They went red to the ears and swore eternal devotion.

Summer, from her ripe wisdom of 13 years, said I was wicked. Perhaps I am. But I cannot help it if men choose to fight over me; it isn't my fault they make such fine entertainment.

"She'd have made a successful courtesan in London," James drawled.

Cecilia nodded and read on. "Oh, here is another good passage from a day or so later:"

It is delicious to be adored.

"That speaks quite pointedly to her character," James said. "I agree, and it gets worse."

I think half the parish is in love with me. If not, they should be.

It amuses me how everyone scurries at my bidding. Such fuss over a few leaves of pennyroyal! Gussie and Martha whispered like conspirators when they gave me their little parcel, as if they were playing at wickedness. Sweet, silly girls.

Haydon stared at me from the brewery's door this morning, all self-importance and scorn. He pretends indifference, but I swear he watches every step I take. He scowls at me as if my

mere presence would burn his beer, yet he fetched some penny-
royal for me all the same. –In secret, of course. He passed a
small canvas bag of pennyroyal to Summer for me.

The Cathcart twins still limp about like wounded heroes,
glaring at one another whenever I pass. They, too, passed
pennyroyal to Summer for me.

I smiled at one of them today, just to see the other's jaw
tighten. One little glance, and they'll be ready to swing again.
Men are absurd creatures—built for my amusement.

"And here is where she talks about Viscount Kendell," Cecilia said. She took another sip of coffee, then wrinkled her nose. "James, can you send for a fresh pot of coffee? This one has gone quite cold."

With her coffee refreshed, Cecilia continued.

As for the Viscount—ah, he plays the grand gentleman, but I
see how his eyes linger. He calls me reckless; I call him dull.
When I am mistress of his fine house, he will thank me for
rescuing him from boredom.

Even my dear brother, George, hovers like a puppy, eager to
please. He fetched me ribbons from town today; said they were
the shade of my eyes. I kissed his cheek, which made him blush
and stammer. My brother is the easiest of all.

If I were to disappear, they'd likely pine themselves to
death.

Cecilia skimmed ahead. "Oh, James, Miss Georgia is beginning to be frightened. It has been a couple of days since the previous entry. I wonder what has happened. I detect bravado in this next entry. Tell me what you think."

I am done being frightened. The stupid talk of "herbs" and "remedies" has gone on long enough. The thing is gone—nature took care of it days ago, though no one but I know that. I hid the evidence and then got rid of it before my maid could discover and tell Mother. She would have told Father and saved him the trouble of pretending concern, but I prefer that he scheme and fret.

"She lost the babe naturally?" James asked.

"That is how I read that," Cecilia said.

"And she didn't want anyone to know. Most interesting."

"The babe was a useful ploy."

He sent Mrs. Hester fussing about her jar containing the pennyroyal again. He said that I must "drink the tea." Well, Mrs. Hester may brew whatever she chooses—I've taken every bit of the pennyroyal from her jar and replaced it with spearmint. They smell near enough alike. If he means to poison me in a mistaken means to regain respectability, he'll only make me feel refreshed.

The Cathcart twins say the apothecary in Maidstone has no more pennyroyal to sell, which pleases me mightily. Let Father rage; he can do nothing now. There is no more pennyroyal to be had. I am safe.

As for the Viscount, he still plays the virtuous man, talking of duty and scandal as though either could bind me—but he said he did try to procure pennyroyal; however, the apothecary in Maidstone was sold out. I shrugged at him and told him no matter, that I will not take it anyway. He says he will not marry me, no matter what.

Not yet, I told him, and smiled. He will yield in time—they always do. Once the vows are said, I shall turn him as easily as I turned the rest into doting devotees.

I am finished being afraid of men. They will all learn it soon enough.

I wonder how much pennyroyal is now in my hiding place. Likely enough to poison the entire village!

Cecilia paused. "Didn't George say he bought pennyroyal in Folkestone, not Maidstone?"

James nodded. "I begin to understand how she came to take the pennyroyal."

"Thinking she was drinking mint tea."

He nodded. "Remember how George said he gave the pennyroyal he'd purchased into his father's care? And not Georgia's or Mrs. Hester's?"

"The magistrate most likely added it to Mrs. Hester's jar."

Kendell is a fool. I told him plainly—if he marries me, all is well, the child will be his, and no one need whisper. It would raise him, not lower me. He had the insolence to laugh and say he will not be "caught" as his father once was. He called me reckless. Reckless! I am giving him the chance of his life. He dares refuse me, saying he won't be "trapped." Trapped! As though any man could do better than me.

He thinks my Father will not compel him. But Father has always had his way, and he will again. I will see the Viscount kneel before me yet, whether by altar or by scandal—child or no child.

Kendell avoids me, but he cannot avoid me forever. Father says it will be arranged, he will see it settled, and I believe him. When he speaks so, I know he means to force the issue. He

*knows I will not be cast aside. I will be mistress of a fine house,
and all these petty folk will curtsy when I pass.*

"She is losing confidence," James observed. "What is the
date on that entry?"

Cecilia looked down at it again. "April 28th."

"Hmm. Five days before she dies," James muses.

Cecilia glances through the next entry. "You are correct. I
believe she's now fearful for her life and living on ego,
bravado, and sheer nerve."

*Father has been rougher as of late. Yesterday, he gripped my
arm so tightly when he shook me that today I am forced to wear
long sleeves to hide the bruises his grip created.*

*And today, all morning, like a broody hen, Mrs. Hester has
been fluttering about my cottage—for so I've come to think of
this shabby, cozy hut. I asked what she was so agitated about.
She said Father ordered her to "see to the herbs." I laughed in her
face. Let him order her to prepare the pennyroyal tea—I
changed the contents of her jar myself. I know every leaf in
there. I told her that and swore her to silence.*

*She gives me sad, pitying looks, as if she knows something I
do not. Poor woman. I can almost feel sorry for her. When I live
after I drink the pennyroyal tea—and since Father knows he
can't control me—he will try to kill me. I'm certain of it. La!
Luckily, I am smarter than he. Mrs. Hester forgets who taught
me to lie with a straight face.*

*I stole a carving knife from the kitchen. I keep it with me,
hidden in the pocket tied on top of my petticoats.*

Mother has a headache this evening. Father dined in his study again. I could hear his voice raised—poor George catching the storm, no doubt. He has been away to Folkestone on some errand for Father, or so Mrs. Hester let slip. I hardly care what fool's errand it was; I only wish he'd grow a spine and tell Father to hang himself.

Tomorrow, perhaps, I'll let Mrs. Hester brew her tea just to see her flutter. I'll drink it before her, make her believe father's plan has worked, and then smile at her when nothing happens. She knows it is spearmint, but she'll fuss even more, twisting her hands together as she does, sure Father will blame her whether I live or die. I choose to live.

Let him try to master me. I am not the one who will fall.

Cecilia laid the book on the desk between them. She touched her fingertips against her lips for a moment, then dropped her hand on top of the book. "This has become terrifying to read!" she told James, her breath catching. "I'm confused as to what Mrs. Hester did and did not know. She and Mrs. Inglewood are the only people we haven't talked to who we should have talked to."

"According to Inglewood, Lady Inglewood has been indisposed with grief—but most likely with fear based on what we are learning about the man," James said.

"Mrs. Hull is a friend of Mrs. Hester's. I'll send a note around to Mrs. Hull to see if she might arrange a meeting with Mrs. Hester later today or early tomorrow so I might speak with her. I should do that right now." She crossed the room to the massive walnut desk and retrieved paper and pen.

James sauntered across the room to stand by her as she wrote. "A secretly arranged meeting is probably the only way you'll get to speak with her if the magistrate is as guilty as we now believe."

Cecilia nodded as she finished the note. James rang the bell for Coggins.

"See that Daniel takes this note to the vicarage immediately and gives it directly to Mrs. Hull. If she isn't there, tell him to find her as he did us yesterday. He is to wait until she reads it and he's to ask if she has any message to send back for Lady Branstoke."

With the note on its way, Cecilia and James returned to the table by the window. Cecilia reopened the diary. She slid her hand down the next diary page, her lips compressing slightly. "Even though we know what happened, this attitude Georgia has toward drinking the tea, and our knowing she was not as clever as she imagined, feels like a fist squeezing my breath away. My eyes threaten tears even though she was alive when she wrote this."

"Do you wish me to take over reading the diary?"

She flipped through the pages and shook her head. "No. I will continue. There is only one more entry remaining."

May 3rd

La! Mrs. Hester finally brought me the tea, and she brought it to the cottage, as I requested. Not to my bedroom. Now this farce will end.

"She didn't know how correct she would prove to be when she wrote that last sentence," Cecilia said sadly.

Her hands are shaking like a servant caught stealing. I told her she needn't look so grim; it's only spearmint, after all. I smiled when I saw the steam curl up—victory smells sweet!

Still...it tastes strange. More bitter than I remember. Not unpleasant, exactly, just different. I teased her, asked if she'd changed her recipe, and she only twisted her hands before her shapeless maroon dress and said Father wished me to drink it all.

"Dear lord, she didn't realize—" She looked up at James, tears suddenly sliding down her cheeks.

James quickly rose from his chair and came over to her, drawing her up into his arms.

"I'm sorry. I knew this happened, but reading it like this… She didn't know…" Cecilia said softly. "My eyes are blurry…"

"I'll finish reading it," James said.

He is in the garden on our property, across the stone wall, pacing, waiting for me to obey. I'll finish the cup, then go to him and tell him what a fool he is—how easily I outwitted him.

Hmm, my stomach is reacting to the bitterness I taste. How much spearmint did Mrs. Hester use to brew this tea? Any tea, in too large a quantity or over-brewed, can taste bitter.

I'm starting to perspire. How odd. My head feels—
Where did he get this?
My stomach

"There is an ink smear after 'stomach' that trails down the page," James told her.

"How could she go on writing as she did once she understood what was happening? She knew she'd been poisoned," Cecilia asked, clinging to James.

"In her way, she was an inordinately strong woman, even if wrong-headed," James said, stroking Cecilia's hair and gently kissing her temple. He wrapped his arms tightly around her, holding her close in silence as her tears fell.

Cecilia reveled in his embrace. It gave her comfort, comfort, and love she felt certain Georgia Inglewood never experienced. She relaxed against him, her eyes closed for a few moments more, then she pulled back and looked up into his beloved face. She smiled up at him. "Thank you," she whispered.

He looked quizzically at her.

"For being you," she said.

He smiled down at her and pulled her close again for a quick hug, then he let her go.

Cecilia swiped at the tears in her eyes and on her cheeks. "Silly me; I knew what we were doing this morning and failed to carry a handkerchief with me," she said with a little laugh.

James reached into his waistcoat pocket. "I didn't," he said. He drew out his handkerchief and handed it to her. He watched her as she wiped away the evidence of her tears.

"Well now," she said, with a bit of forced calmness, "we have much to do today. I am glad I read the journal before my encounter with Mrs. Hester. I'm certain Mrs. Hester knows the magistrate's role in his daughter's death."

"She's likely terrified," James warned her.

"I know, I shall have to question her carefully. I do not want the magistrate to suspect she has told us anything—if she does."

"She will. She won't be able to resist you," James assured her.

"Please don't say that. It reminds me too much of Georgia."

Cecilia drew in a deep breath and let it out. "As I wait to hear from Mrs. Hull, I'm going upstairs to spend some time with Hugh. I need to hold my son against me and relish in his life."

James nodded. "I will see you later. I'm going to see if I can talk to George again. I would hazard that he will be at the tavern. He won't return to Folkestone until after Mrs. Jones's burial."

CHAPTER 14

THE INGLEWOOD HOUSEHOLD

James stopped at the door of the Sheep's Head Tavern. He smiled slightly and found a certain sympathy within himself for the young man sitting at the bar, a mug of coffee before him. He walked up to the stool next to him and pulled it out.

"I'm somehow gratified to see you are not indulging in spirits at this early hour," he said as he sat down next to Mr. George Inglewood. He motioned to Mr. Hopkins that he'd like a coffee as well.

Mr. Inglewood had forgone his cravat, his shirt open at the neck; however, all other aspects of his attire were pressed and neat. He turned his head and nodded to James. "Good morning. I'm surprised to see you at this fine establishment so early in the day," he said, gesturing with his hand to encompass the entire, empty tavern.

"I was looking for you. I had a notion I might find you here," James said calmly. He nodded his thanks to Mr. Hopkins when that worthy passed him a glass mug of coffee.

Steam curled up from the hot brew. He lightly placed his hands around the mug.

"Looking for me? I'm the least person in this village. What could you want with me?" he asked despondently.

James frowned slightly. "Why do you call yourself the least person? You're the son of the local squire and magistrate."

He barked a humorless laugh. "I would that I wasn't."

"Having had some dealings with your father over Mrs. Jones' death, I would hazard a guess your discontent stems from him."

His shoulders slumped. "You have that right."

"May I ask you a question?"

"Ask away." George stared into his mug.

James kept his expression neutral, his tone flat. "Is your father cruel?"

George's head jerked up. "Why would you ask that?"

"Your sister's friends told my wife of seeing bruises on her," he told him matter-of-factly.

George looked at him. In his eyes, James thought he saw conflicting thoughts racing. Finally, he breathed out as if he'd been holding his breath for a long time.

"That's true," he finally said. He shifted on his stool to face James. "He liked to squeeze her arm or her hand until she couldn't help but whimper in pain."

"Did you never try to stop him?"

"Once I did to him what he did to her—my hands are strong from pulling ropes on the yacht," he stated, holding his hands in front of himself and looking at them. "I squeezed his arm so tightly that he bruised, as my sister did. I told him that was how his behavior felt to Georgia, and it was too much, too vicious. And you know what he did afterward? He thanked me. Thanked me! He did not thank me so he would stop; he thanked me so he could know what level of pain he caused her!"

"Why didn't you report him to Mortlake, or the magistrate in Folkestone?"

"What could Mortlake do? He might be the highest-ranking aristocrat in the area, but my father is the magistrate. And what would the magistrate in Folkestone do? He's a virtual pirate! Smuggling goods from Europe to England!" George said, his voice now agitated. When he settled down, he continued. "Besides, a man can do anything he wants to his family as punishment short of killing them," he finished bitterly.

James stared at George for a moment, then picked up his mug and sipped his coffee. "But he did kill your sister," he stated calmly, softly.

George looked at him silently for a moment, then he started to cry. "Yes," he whispered.

"Tell me about it," James encouraged him. "You will feel better for doing so."

He shook his head. "No, I won't. I told Mrs. Jones, and look what happened to her. I can't have a third death on my soul."

"Third?" James queried.

"My sister, Mrs. Jones, and you," he ground out.

James shook his head. "He won't kill me, and you are not responsible for the deaths of your sister and Mrs. Jones."

"I am!" He buried his face in his hands as he sobbed.

James passed his handkerchief to him and slid some coins onto the bar. "Come. Come with me," James urged him. He pulled him up and guided him toward the door.

"What are you doing? Where are we going?" George asked.

"To Summerworth Park," James said. "Hiding in a bar all day is not healthy, even if you only drink coffee. That would change eventually. And returning to your home, where your father can question your activities, is not advised. You look as if you haven't slept in days. You need rest. Come with me. We will put it about that you have volunteered to help prepare for the gathering tomorrow after Mrs. Jones' burial."

George came willingly enough, though his steps were slow. As they walked to Summerworth Park, James wondered how he might use what he had learned to have the magistrate arrested.

NOT AN HOUR after she sent the note off to Mrs. Hull, Cecilia received a response. "Thank you, Daniel," Cecilia absently murmured as she shifted Hugh's weight to her hip and took the note from Daniel. She saw that Mrs. Hull had dashed off her response on the backside of the note Cecilia had sent to her.

> *Dear Lady Branstoke,*
>
> *By previous arrangement, and now lucky happenstance, Mrs. Hester is coming to the vicarage today at 4:00 p.m. to join me for tea. Please join us. I suggest you arrive sometime shortly after 4:00 for a <u>surprise</u> visit.*
>
> *The Vicar is at Mortlake House. I'm hoping that is a good thing.*
>
> *Sincerely,*
> *Mrs. Hull*

Cecilia took Hugh to her dressing room and laid him on a blanket on the floor, then rang for Sarah. Hugh fussed and kicked his feet angrily, his face contorting into discomfort and tears. Cecilia sat down on the floor and pulled him into her lap. "Your mouth is hurting. I know, little love. I'll ask Sarah to fetch a biscuit. You can gnaw on that until nap time," she told him, rubbing his back to soothe him.

"Yes, my lady?" Sarah said from the doorway.

"Please get one of Mrs. Rutledge's biscuits for Hugh. When you return, we will discuss a visit I must make today for which I would like your company and assistance."

SARAH SAT WIDE-EYED and aghast at all Cecilia told her about what Sir James and she had learned from Miss Inglewood's diary. Sarah readily agreed with Cecilia that it was imperative that they speak with Mrs. Hester. Cecilia and Sarah agreed that getting her to speak to them about what she knew might prove difficult. Sarah suggested that she coax the woman to talk while Cecilia held Mrs. Hull in conversation. This would help put the woman at ease. Sarah could tell Mrs. Hester that Cecilia had found and read the diary. Hopefully, Mrs. Hester would want to know what was in the diary, and she would be the one to first ask a question of Cecilia. If she initiated the conversation, she would be more inclined to keep asking questions about the journal and, with the right gentle prodding, continue the conversation by offering what she knew or had seen.

At four o'clock, after giving Hugh one last kiss and handing him over to Mary Alice, Cecilia left Summerworth with Sarah as her companion for propriety, and they walked the half mile to the vicarage.

"Lady Branstoke," Mrs. Hull enthused when she answered the door to her knock. "Come in, come in, please."

"Is the vicar here?" Cecilia asked loudly as she crossed the threshold.

Mrs. Hull smiled, and replied equally loudly, "No, he be up at the Mortlake House, visiting his daughters."

"I'm sorry to miss him, but delighted to hear his daughters are talking to him."

"As am I. But come into the parlor. Mrs. Hester is here for tea, and since you've walked here from Summerworth, you should join us. You as well, Sarah," Mrs. Hull said.

When they walked into the parlor, Mrs. Hester looked like she was preparing to leave. "I—I should go," she said to Mrs. Hull, "now that Lady Branstoke is here."

"Not at all," Cecilia said. "Please, you were here before me and enjoying a comfortable coze with Mrs. Hull. Far be it for me to disturb that."

"But you are a lady and I—"

"Pshaw. I wasn't always, you know. For eight years, I was married to a merchant. I am no longer comfortable with society's class rules. Let me introduce you to Sarah, my lady's maid, companion, and friend. She has seen me through some wild experiences."

"That I have," Sarah agreed. "I could tell you some stories…" Her voice shifted to a shared secrets tone as she sat down next to Mrs. Hester.

"How was the vicar this morning?" Cecilia asked as she accepted a cup of tea from Mrs. Hull. She kept one ear tuned to hints of the conversation occurring between Sarah and Mrs. Hester.

"Very well, when I arrived here this morning and practically giddy after breakfast when he received a note requesting he come to Mortlake House for the day."

In the background, Cecilia heard Sarah commiserating with Mrs. Hester over the loss of Miss Inglewood and now Mrs. Jones.

"Did he tell you how it came about that they are talking?" Cecilia asked Mrs. Hull.

"Something about rearranged seating cards at dinner?"

Cecilia laughed. "Yes. Before dinner, I snuck into the dining room and did some careful seating rearrangement. Lady Mortlake was quite put out with me when she discovered what I'd done."

"I imagine so. She is an amiable woman, for a countess, but a bit starchy."

Cecilia reached over and patted her hand. "Comes with the title."

"I know. So tell me exactly what you did."

"I put the vicar in the middle of the table with one of the girls on either side of him, and on either side of them, I placed Lord Aldrich and my husband. Then I coached Lord Aldrich and my husband to ask them questions about childhood memories of growing up at the vicarage. This forced them to recall happy times with the vicar as their father, and had the vicar entering into the conversation, recalling events. There was soon a great deal of laughter from that side of the table, I am happy to relate. Soon, everyone became involved in listening to the tales and laughing all around the table—quite against society dinner protocol, but something beneficial for the Vicar as well as his daughters."

"Well done, my lady!" Mrs. Hester enthused as they heard from the sofa where Sarah and Mrs. Hester sat, "She found it?! Where? What did it say?"

"I have not read it. You will have to ask Lady Branstoke," Sarah encouraged, just as she and Cecilia had arranged.

Cecilia winked at Mrs. Hull, hoping she would take the hint to be quiet for a moment as she sipped her tea.

"Lady Branstoke?" Mrs. Hester said, her voice high and uncertain. "Lady Branstoke, Sarah tells me you found Georgia's diary?"

"The one she hid in the old gatekeeper's cottage? Yes," Cecilia said, hoping to draw her out to ask more questions. Next to her, Mrs. Hull looked like a bright little bird, her dark eyes jumping from her to Mrs. Hester and back.

"Where? I looked everywhere. I was afraid…" Her voice trailed off.

"What? That the magistrate would find it?" Cecilia asked.

"Yes— No! Worse…" Color suffused her cheeks. "That someone else would find it."

"Why would either circumstance be a concern?" Cecilia asked in a calm, gentle, manner.

Mrs. Hester licked her lips. "The squire and his daughter did not get along," she finally, carefully said. "She may have written things that would make him angry or make others gossip."

"You mean like the fact that he beat her?" Cecilia asked, leaning forward.

Mrs. Hull inhaled sharply.

Mrs. Hester's lips quivered. "You know," she whispered. She looked down.

"Yes, and I surmise he beats his wife as well, which is why we so seldom see Lady Alfred Inglewood at church on Sundays."

"Yes," whispered Mrs. Hester, her eyes filling with unshed tears.

"Poor woman," Mrs. Hull murmured.

"In her diary, Miss Inglewood seemed assured she could manipulate her father to do as she wished him to do," Cecilia continued. "However, something must have happened close to the day she died." Her expression grew pensive. "Suddenly, she became convinced her father wanted her dead, and she started carrying a large butcher knife hidden in her skirts."

Mrs. Hester's face crumpled as she fought—and lost—against tears streaming down her cheeks. Sarah handed her a handkerchief.

"Oddly, though she'd begun to seriously fear him, she still thought she would win him over. Whatever happened is not in her diary. Do you know what occurred that had her believing he would kill her?"

"He told her that if she did not drink that tea, he would kill her, for he would not accept a pregnant trollop for a daughter."

Cecilia compressed her lips as she shook her head. "Did you know that she lost the child without drinking the pennyroyal tea?"

Mrs. Hester stopped dabbing at her tears and looked stunned at Cecilia. "What? No!"

"She wrote of it in her diary, and also said she didn't want anyone to know yet. She still hoped to use the child as leverage to get the viscount to marry her."

"Why didn't she tell me! Why didn't she tell the squire?"

Cecilia sighed. "From what Sir James and I could infer from what she wrote, she replaced the pennyroyal in the canister in the kitchen with spearmint. She said they smelled similar and no one would know. She could drink that tea and then confront her father to show him she yet lived."

"I knew about the spearmint, but the squire seemed so confident of her death I didn't know what to think. I served her that cursed brew, whatever it was, and watched her take sick. Later, after the young master carried Miss Georgia to her room, he came to me crying. Miss Georgia told him, between her cries of pain as he carried her, that it was supposed to be spearmint in the canister and there was no more pennyroyal to be had in Maidstone. Guilt consumed him for he'd purchased pennyroyal in Folkestone and gave it to his father. The squire must have put it in the canister. And that is what I made her tea with. I killed her!"

"You did not know. It is not your fault," Mrs. Hull said. "Do not be blaming yourself."

"You are as much a victim as Miss Inglewood," Sarah said. She put her arm around the sobbing Mrs. Hester.

Cecilia listened to Mrs. Hull and Sarah console Mrs. Hester. It was understandable that the woman would feel burdened and responsible for what happened. How could she have kept that guilt bottled within her for so long? No, she probably hadn't.

"Is this the first time you have spoken about this?" Cecilia asked

Mrs. Hester shook her head. "I was so confused and heart sick. I had to talk to someone."

Cecilia nodded. "You confessed all that you knew to Mrs. Jones, didn't you?"

Mrs. Hester nodded. "Yes, but I never considered that she would confront the squire."

A cold shiver ran down Cecilia's spine. Knowing Squire Inglewood's violent nature, imagined scenes of Mrs. Jones confronting Inglewood played in her mind as vividly as her most vivid dreams.

"When did she confront the squire?" Cecilia asked.

"Two days before she died," Mrs. Hester said, sniffing.

Two days, Cecilia considered. "The squire and his daughter were much alike," she said slowly. "They were both detailed planners; the squire is still a planner."

"Yes."

"They both considered themselves smarter and more clever than those around them."

"That is true!" offered Mrs. Hull vehemently. Mrs. Hester looked pained.

Cecilia smiled at Mrs. Hull. "And I hazard a guess that they did not like being mocked or ignored. We could see this in Georgia through her diary. From her comments in her diary and what I have seen of our magistrate, I would venture they are alike in this manner as well."

"Yes. Their pride strode before them," Mrs. Hull said drily.

"But they are smarter than those around them," Mrs. Hester insisted. "Others should listen to what they have to say."

"Why?" Cecilia countered.

"I—I..." Mrs. Hester looked confused.

"Being smart does not grant a person wisdom. Nor does it make a person right one hundred percent of the time."

"Aye, and in my time, I have seen a smart person brought low by someone they judged inferior to them," Mrs. Hull said.

"Successful smart people have their intelligence tempered with humility," Cecilia explained.

"Pride cometh before a fall," Sarah murmured.

"Did the squire know Mrs. Jones often went up into the downs to paint?" Cecilia asked.

"Yes. Everyone in the village did," Mrs. Hester replied.

"It is likely that the squire followed her up onto the downs and threatened her in some way to keep her tongue between her teeth and not spread stories of what she suspected had happened to Georgia."

"Gossip would anger him," Mrs. Hester said, frowning.

Cecilia nodded. "That is my expectation as well. Unfortunately, we have no way of proving that the magistrate was instrumental in Georgia's death or in Mrs. Jones death. However, rumor might," Cecilia said.

"What do you mean?" Mrs. Hull asked.

"We," Cecilia said, indicating the four of them in the vicar's parlor, "know the magistrate is culpable in the deaths of his daughter and Mrs. Jones, but we lack proof. What do you suppose might happen if these deaths were discussed in the village with doubts raised?"

Sarah smiled, her eyes bright. "Gossip!" she declared.

"Yes. The village loves to gossip. What if we carefully feed it bits of gossip, bits from Georgia's diary, and other ideas at the gathering after her funeral?"

"It would go around like a wildfire; however, how can that help us entrap Squire Inglewood?"

"I'll ask the vicar to give a sermon on the evils of gossip on Sunday and have him say that I have read Miss Inglewood's diary, and he can ask me to come forward to share with the congregation what Miss Inglewood wrote. I will try to demur, but he will insist, and I will reluctantly read from the diary."

"The squire will protest, say that it is an invasion of family privacy or some such. Or claim that what you're reading is fake," Mrs. Hester said.

"I expect him to. I doubt any will believe him and will want to hear from the diary."

Mrs. Hester nodded slowly. "He will anger quickly and not be overly cautious with his words."

"That is what I am hoping."

"What gossip are we to share?" Mrs. Hull asked. "And how are we to share it?"

"I brought her diary with me," Cecilia said, opening her reticule and drawing out the book. "We can start with what she wrote. Mrs. Hull, can you get paper and a pen or pencil that we can note down what we want to slyly share?"

"The vicar has some in his study. I'm sure he won't mind us using some," she said, getting up to fetch the items.

"Do you think this will work?" Sarah asked.

Mrs. Hester thought a moment, wiped away the last of her tears, and nodded. "I know the squire the best, and knowing him, I think it will. He is prideful. He will not stay silent."

"And I'm hoping it will get Lady Alfred Inglewood to speak up," Cecilia said.

"Let's start with the bit of gossip Summer Rutledge told me that I found confirmed in the diary." She opened the diary, flipping through the pages. "All right. Here it is…"

CHAPTER 15

A BURIAL AND A GATHERING

James informed Cecilia that the vicar had scheduled his wife's burial for one o'clock in the afternoon.

"Why in the afternoon?"

"From my understanding, her daughters want to see her and fasten her dancing sisters cameo at her neck."

"They've forgiven their mother!" Cecilia exclaimed.

"I assume so, for the vicar appeared happy early this morning when I went by the church to check on the pulpit rebuild."

"Good. Have enough pallbearers been recruited?"

James laughed. "There was no recruiting; there are more than enough volunteers. Mrs. Jones was well-liked and greatly missed."

"I count on our plans for Squire Inglewood incriminating himself tomorrow to work," Cecilia said, determination reflected in her expression.

"From what you have told me of your plans and my observations of Squire Inglewood, I know you have a high chance of success."

"We have ensured that the entire parish is aware of the gathering here, and it is here because you are the acting church warden and sexton until replacements are named."

"Ah, that is another piece of good news. The vicar said he received condolences from the Archbishop yesterday. With the letter of condolence came his approval for a curate. In addition, he told the vicar that he needed to press the parish board to fill the churchwarden and sexton roles. The tithes defend the expense."

"That is good news! But we'll have to convince the vicar not to ask Mrs. Hull to move into the middle almshouse and give her residence to a new curate. She likes her end location."

James' eyes narrowed. "I'm not satisfied with the latitude the earl has allowed Inglewood. I suspect Inglewood is holding something over him. I will request Mortlake to build a curate's residence as a thank you," he suggested, his lips kicking up on one side.

Cecilia's eyes lit up. "I agree with you. There is something. Didn't the earl say that they were at the university together for one year? Perhaps Inglewood knows of another indiscretion. Regardless of what it is, I imagine he will be amenable to that idea. Wonderful notion. Mention a new curate's residence to him when he is here this afternoon. With the parish invited, it will be easy to see the need for a curate."

"*If* a large portion of the parish comes, not simply the landed gentry," James cautioned.

"Mrs. Hull believes they will. And with that in mind, I need to meet with Mrs. Vernon now to review our plans for food and drink for the event. I have to tell you, I laughed when she

told me she informed her nephew he was supplying the ale—
for free."

THIS WAS one day when James felt grateful for his acting
churchwarden duties. Those duties kept him at the church
while village men carried Mrs. Jones' casket to her final place
of rest. He didn't do well with burials. Dying soldiers and
burials brought back too many memories of Spain, memories
that caused sleepless nights. He'd suffered the night after he'd
found Mrs. Jones. Today, if he stayed away from the actual
burial, he might save himself another restless night. He saw
the funeral procession stop by the new grave. He turned
away before they lowered her casket. He entered the church
office and methodically recorded the official date of death,
the date of burial, and the other details wanted in the church
record.

When he came out of the office, he found Squire Inglewood standing by the church, watching the burial. He turned
at the sound of James's approach.

"You're not with the funeral party," he noted.

"No," James said.

"Why not? I thought Mrs. Jones was a particular friend of
yours and Lady Branstoke's."

"I could ask you the same question in reverse. Why are you
here? It is known you were not fond of Mrs. Jones."

"Meddlesome woman didn't know her place. Poking her
nose where it did not belong. Spreading gossip…"

"She did much for the parish and was well liked," James
countered. "So, again, why are you here?"

"Not for that witch. I figured you would be here. I came to see you."

"Me?" James crossed his arms over his chest and canted his head as he regarded the squire.

"Stay away from my son," Inglewood growled, his hands clenched at his sides.

"Stay away from George? I have encountered him twice, both times at the Sheep's Head Tavern. A public place."

"You took him to your estate and got him doing servants' labor."

"I do not understand you, Inglewood."

"He came home last evening with tales of sweeping a terrace, hauling tables, and other demeaning work an Inglewood does not do!"

"The night before, I had been asked to hold the gathering for Mrs. Jones. Nothing at our estate was ready for that task. George asked to help my wife, me, and our staff ready the estate. We all worked, and I did not ask him to; he volunteered."

"He's too young to know better. I made sure to address that problem last night," Inglewood said.

"What did you do, beat him?" James asked calmly.

Inglewood's nostrils flared with anger. "You, sir, are impertinent," he said loudly.

James shrugged. "Your son is a fine young man, a man with a desire for friendship and approval. You should be proud of him, not condemning."

Inglewood bristled. "He needs to learn the Inglewood place in society, and it is not doing menial tasks or playing at sea captain. Stay away from him or else!"

Behind Inglewood, James saw those by the gravesite turn in their direction as the squire raised his voice.

"Or else what?" James dropped his arms to his sides. He did not like Inglewood, but did not desire to get into an altercation on church holy grounds. Nonetheless, he would not slink away as many in the town did, and Inglewood appeared to expect.

"You forget I am the magistrate here."

"I forget nothing; however, I do fail to understand what you being the local magistrate has to do with this conversation," James returned. His voice assumed a harder, though still quiet, tone.

"I will have you arrested and thrown into my gaol!" Inglewood yelled at him.

"On trumped-up charges, as you did to Mr. Vernon?"

"Everything all right here?" Aldrich called out as he walked back from the cemetery.

Inglewood swung around. The burial finished, the men were making their way back toward the church.

Inglewood swung back toward James. "I am not finished with you," he growled.

James raised an eyebrow. Inglewood sneered and stalked away toward Inglewood Manor.

"What was that about?" Aldrich asked James as he came up beside him.

"Inglewood told me to stay away from his son. I believe he thinks me a bad influence on him."

Aldrich barked a laugh. "You? A bad influence? The Peninsular War hero? The righter of wrongs and purveyor of justice, a bad influence?"

James relaxed. He smiled at his friend. "The righter of

wrongs and purveyor of justice is my wife, I merely follow where she leads."

Aldrich clapped him on his back and laughed louder. Together, they walked to Summerworth Park and James told him about the diary contents.

"I believe it," Aldrich said, nodding. "But that wouldn't stand up before a judge as evidence."

"We know. We need him to incriminate himself."

Lord Aldrich frowned. "How do you intend to do that?"

"Gossip. At the gathering, it will become known that Cecilia and I have found and read Miss Inglewood's diary."

"And you intend to share information from the diary?"

James nodded slowly. "And what we have learned through our investigation."

"What would that be?"

"The pennyroyal was kept in a canister in the kitchen."

"That's macabre," Aldrich said, his mouth twisting in distaste.

"I quite agree. However, there it sat. At some point, days before she died, Miss Inglewood removed the pennyroyal and replaced it with spearmint."

"She did not want to get rid of the child she carried?"

"She'd lost it, but didn't tell anyone."

"Why not?"

"She thought she could pressure Kendell to marry her. She also wanted her father to pressure him as well, which he wouldn't do if she were not with child."

"If she changed the canister contents to spearmint, how did she die?"

"Pennyroyal."

"What?"

"Inglewood told his son to go to Folkestone to see if he could get pennyroyal for his sister. When he returned, he gave it to his father."

"And his father placed it in the canister."

James nodded. "Inglewood wanted his daughter to die."

"No!"

"Oh, yes. And Miss Inglewood knew it. When the pot was brewed, she thought she would triumph over her father and show him she was perfectly healthy. She saw that as some kind of revenge on her father. He wanted to control everyone in his family, and she wasn't having that. She wanted to hurt him, hurt his pride."

"They had odd family relations."

"Yes. We know from the diary that Inglewood did inflict pain if he didn't get his way. Cecilia and I imagine that is why Lady Inglewood does not come to Sunday services often, for the bruises she needs to hide."

"You consider making this information public will cause him to reveal himself?"

"That is the plan. I do not expect it will happen as swiftly as Cecilia does, but eventually, he will break. You saw him at the church. He was angry with me because George helped us prepare the estate for today's gathering. Said it was beneath an Inglewood."

"He does think well of himself."

"And will attempt to use his magistrate role to punish me," James said drolly as they approached the front door of Summerworth.

"I assume I am to share these revelations?" Aldrich asked as they entered the manor.

"In a *keep-this-to-yourself* manner."

Aldrich rubbed his hands together, his eyes laughing. "But, of course!"

CECILIA HAD BEEN CORRECT, James mused some ninety minutes later as he looked around the throng in his house and spilling out across the terrace and into Cecilia's garden. The parish had come to honor Mrs. Jones and give condolences to the vicar and to Hope and Faith Jones. He almost wished Inglewood was present to see the attendance and the stories exchanged about her many kindnesses. Then again, not, for then the stories of his family and his perfidy would not have been shared. And his perfidy was being shared. He saw it in the faces of those who learned of it, the frowns, the anger.

He walked through the rooms of his house and out onto the terrace, exchanging solemn nods and condolences. He felt pleased with the appearance of the house after its two years of renovations. It did not have ornate rooms like the earl had in his manor; nonetheless, it was beautiful. They'd done well.

Per prior agreement with Cecilia, neither he nor she mentioned the diary or what they knew. They let those they had told ahead of the gathering carry that torch forward.

He knew their plan had been successful when the Earl of Mortlake approached him on the terrace.

"A word, Sir James," Mortlake said, coming up to him, a mug of ale in hand. "I heard you have possession of a diary of Miss Inglewood's."

"It is actually Lady Branstoke who claims the diary," James corrected.

"Are you certain it is hers and not something planted to cause problems in Mertonhaugh?"

"We are confident it is authentic," James replied.

"Why have you not returned it to the family?"

James stared at him for a long moment. "You know we have it, but not its contents," he finally said.

"I did not stay to listen. I want to know what this is about. It appears people are gossiping about it and not thinking of Mr. Jones," the earl complained.

"I assure you, they are doing both. I have heard them. Come. I will let you see for yourself."

He led Mortlake to his modest library and shut the door behind them. Only a single lamp, turned low, sat in the room. James brought it forward and turned up its light. He then walked to his desk and unlocked a drawer to draw out the book. "Here," he said. "I suggest you start on April 23rd. It shouldn't take you long."

Mortlake looked at him, frowning, but sat down in a wing chair by the fireplace. James walked to the beverage sideboard. "Brandy?" he asked.

Mortlake nodded.

James poured the brandy for each of them, then sat in the chair opposite Mortlake to enjoy his brandy and wait.

Fifteen minutes later, Mortlake looked up.

"Did you know," James asked, "Mrs. Jones was not satisfied with the coroner's verdict of iliac passion for Miss Inglewood's cause of death?"

"Yes, she told me. I advised her to let it be. The poor girl was dead, and there was no sense in stirring things up now."

"Mrs. Jones did not take your advice. She took on an

investigator's role and proceeded to question everyone and everything, as Cecilia and I have done. When she spoke to Mrs. Hester, she learned how Miss Inglewood actually died. She concluded that Inglewood was responsible. She confronted him."

"What?" Mortlake said, sitting straighter.

James nodded. "That much Mrs. Hester does know, but not what went on between them; however, two days later, Mrs. Jones went over the cliff from Haughton Meadow."

Horror dawned on Mortlake's face. "You don't think…"

"We do." He spread his hands out in front of himself. "But we have no proof."

"He'll never be brought to justice," Mortlake said.

"Why not?" James asked. He retrieved the brandy bottle from the sideboard and offered the earl another glass. Mortlake accepted.

"People are afraid of him. He has too much on them."

"Like he has on you?" James asked calmly. He took a sip of brandy and then sat back down.

"What are you talking about?"

"You have been protecting him. You have turned your head away from his actions that hurt others, like claiming unpaid taxes and excess taxes due from the district. Those, by the way, are some truths that have come out since people took to talking about the diary. The only time you confronted Inglewood was when he arrested Vernon. That hit too close to you. How much did you pay Inglewood to make that false accusation go away?"

"Fifty pounds," Mortlake admitted.

"I'd call that cheap. You knew, didn't you, that he beat his daughter. Kendell told you. He'd seen the bruises."

"Yes, but there was nothing I could do about that."

James shook his head. "Nothing you chose to do about it. Because he knew something about you that you did not want revealed."

Mortlake's jaw clenched. "Yes, damn, you."

"Something from your university days."

"How did you know?"

James shrugged. "I don't. I'm merely surmising based on what I know and have witnessed."

Mortlake laughed harshly. "It is no wonder people say you are a good investigator."

"I have never set out to be an investigator; unfortunately, I have an incurable curiosity about the world around me, as does Cecilia. You should ask her sometime how we met," he said with a half smile. "Now, what does Inglewood have on you? Perhaps I can help."

"We shared one year at university together and became friends—if you can believe that. I was wild—first time out from under my father's thumb. We decided to steal things, not for money, but to prove we could get away with it. We left what we stole elsewhere to be recovered. Most of the time, the items were recovered. A few times, they were not, for someone else took them. One of the items we took was the chalice cup from the university chapel. It was later found in the possession of Lewis Martin, the illegitimate son of the Earl of Harleigh. He was subsequently expelled, though he protested his innocence. Said he had found it and was going to return it."

"Lewis Martin!" James half rose out of his chair.

"You know him?"

James laughed. "He was a Bow Street agent for many years. Our paths have crossed."

Mortlake looked at him with surprise. "He always was a smart devil, though much younger than the rest of us," he mused.

"So that is what Inglewood has over you? That you let an innocent man take the blame for a theft you committed and be expelled for it? I'm sure it has never bothered Inglewood."

"No, but it has bothered me, and it is something I've never wanted Clementina to know."

"So you let Inglewood hold that over your head. You're a sapskull, Mortlake. You did not harm Mr. Martin by your failure to tell the truth. You probably did him a favor, and I'd wager he knows who committed the thefts. He was later reinstated, you know."

"No, I didn't."

"He went on to study law. He had a desire to be a barrister; however, since he was illegitimate, he was barred from that profession. That's why he joined Bow Street. Tell Lady Mortlake, and dissolve this fear you carry. We need your assistance to make Squire Inglewood as uncomfortable as possible. Our plans won't work if the highest-ranked citizen in the area doesn't take a stand against this man and what he does."

Mortlake picked the diary up off his lap and handed it over to James. "I can't let that young woman's death, nor Mrs. Jones's death, go unresolved."

"Lady Branstoke and I thank you. As he did not come to this gathering nor allow any of his family to attend, we expect Squire Inglewood to learn of the gossip at church tomorrow. –And speaking of what will be learned tomorrow, the Archbishop has approved a curate for the parish. As penance, you are expected to build him a residence."

"Penance?"

"For tolerating Inglewood's behavior."

Mortlake bowed his head. "Accepted."

CHAPTER 16

SUNDAY

*D*uring the Vicar's church service on Sunday, Cecilia did not have to look toward the Inglewood pew box to know Squire Inglewood glared at her. She felt it.

James reached over to gently squeeze her hand. She looked up at him and smiled. They expected a confrontation with the squire when the service ended. The parish must have too, for people filled the pew boxes and crowded the standing room at the back of the church. The attendance would have gratified the vicar if he hadn't known why the crowd gathered, he told Cecilia and James before services began. Cecilia felt guilty that the confrontation with Inglewood would occur on holy ground, a place of peace. And she knew there would be a confrontation; it was in that glare and the set of his jaw.

Cecilia took in a deep breath and exhaled. Her shoulders relaxed as she returned her attention to Vicar Jones, where her attention should have been the entire time.

"I have good news to share," the vicar was saying. "The Archbishop has approved the addition of a curate for our parish. Lord Mortlake and our bishop will begin the process of selection. In addition, Lord Mortlake will see a residence is constructed for our new curate."

There was a murmur throughout the congregation at the news, taking the minds of all off the Inglewood rumors. Cecilia saw that as a good conclusion to the service, easing the tension she'd felt since she'd taken her seat in their box.

The vicar gave the final blessing and said, "Go in peace," signaling the end of the service. The congregants hurried to leave the church; however, they did not leave the church property; they huddled in groups, whispering.

James and Cecilia exited with the Aldriches, stopping to shake the vicar's hand. "Don't worry so," Cecilia said softly. "Everything will be fine."

The vicar looked beyond them to where the Inglewoods followed. "I trust you are right. I place it in God's hands."

James and Cecilia walked away from the church entrance, stopping every few steps to answer queries about the rumors that had flooded the village.

"Sir James!" called out Inglewood, pushing his way through the people before him to catch up with the Branstokes. His wife and son hurried after him.

"I want my daughter's diary," he yelled, his face red. "You have no right to it!"

"Father," George tried to intervene.

Inglewood shoved his son away. George stumbled and fell backward. "Stay out of this," Inglewood growled.

Mr. Altman, the butcher, helped George to his feet.

"Give me that diary!" Inglewood demanded.

"I do not have it upon my person," James said calmly.

Cecilia stepped closer to her husband. "Why do you want

it?" Cecilia asked. "You have the diary she kept in her bedroom. You used to sneak into her room to read it."

"I am her father!"

"And as her father, you had the right to inflict bruises on her?" Cecilia heard a sharp intake of breath from Lady Inglewood, her face hidden behind a veil, and more murmurs from those around them.

"She shamed the Inglewood name. She was a willful whore and deserved what happened to her."

"Is that why you killed her?"

"I didn't kill her, you stupid woman—"

"Easy, Inglewood," James warned, his voice low, a drawn rapier.

"It was that bloody pennyroyal!"

"Your daughter wrote in her diary that she had emptied the canister of pennyroyal and replaced it with spearmint. She knew the apothecary in Maidstone had sold out his supply of pennyroyal, so *you* sent your son to Folkestone to buy more there. You put the pennyroyal in the canister. You ordered Mrs. Hester to brew the pennyroyal and take it to her in the old gamekeeper's cottage while you waited in your garden for events to unfold."

The crowd of parishioners gathered tighter around them, their voices louder. Inglewood glanced at the growing crowd.

"Georgia had lost the child. She had no need of an abortifacient," Cecilia continued, "but she encouraged her friends and family to buy pennyroyal for her. That was her drama, for she still hoped to convince the viscount to marry her."

"It was never going to happen," yelled Kendell from where he stood with the Earl and Countess of Mortlake. Lord Mortlake shushed him.

"After she died, you refused to let Dr. Patterson examine her body, and you somehow persuaded the coroner to pronounce her cause of death as iliac passion. You couldn't let her death be pronounced suicide, for that would mar the Inglewood name. You didn't understand your daughter well. Everyone who knew her knew she was not the sort to commit suicide."

"But Mrs. Jones knew," James said, picking up the narrative with strong certainty. "She already knew of the bruises your daughter and your wife bore from your hand."

"That is family business. That witch poked her nose where it didn't belong."

"She started asking questions, difficult questions about the past and present. People confessed to her as they would to her husband. What she learned angered her, and she confronted you."

"She had no proof, and neither do you. What judge will lend credence to the written words of a mentally deranged young woman?"

"But Mrs. Jones kept pressing, didn't she? Every time she saw you."

Inglewood's hands clenched at his sides.

"One day, you followed her as she went up on the downs to paint. You wanted to talk to her, threaten her, as you did others, to keep her mouth closed. You needed to do this away from a village of prying ears and easy gossip."

"She refused to understand. She wouldn't listen!"

"You grabbed her around her neck, didn't you? That's when her pin came off. What did it do? Scratch you, and you let her go, giving her time to run away from you. Unfortunately, she ran toward the cliff."

"No! I wanted her to listen to me. But she kept ranting on about how I was responsible for my daughter's death. She didn't understand Georgia had to die!" He pulled a gun from his pocket.

Screams erupted. James pushed Cecilia aside. George leaped for his father's gun hand as he fired at the Branstokes, the bullet digging a path into the dirt. Lady Inglewood flung herself at her husband. In an instant, his expression changed from fury to surprise. A heartbeat later, Lady Inglewood stepped back, her hand releasing the hilt of a large carving knife. Blood spurted out of his side. Inglewood's head turned slightly to look at her, then he crumbled to the ground.

Lady Inglewood stared at him, and fainted.

DR. PATTERSON CAME FORWARD to see to Inglewood, while George, at the vicar's instruction, carried Lady Inglewood into the vicarage. Cecilia hurried after them. She pumped water over a cloth she found in the kitchen, wrung it out, and went back to Lady Inglewood, who George had laid on the vicar's sofa.

"Take off her hat and veil," Cecilia directed George. Cecilia gasped when she looked at her, but quickly placed the cool cloth on her head. The squire's wife had a black eye and a deep gash in her cheek.

George pointed to the gash. "That's from my father's signet ring," he said flatly. "I don't know how he caused the black eye."

Cecilia looked at him, shocked, more for how he told her than what he told her. She turned back to Lady Inglewood and dabbed the cloth across her brow and down her neck. Lady Inglewood moaned as she roused from her faint. She blinked her eyes. "Lady Branstoke?" she said weakly. "He didn't shoot you?"

"No, he didn't, thanks to you and your son," she said gently.

"Good…good…" She closed her eyes again.

"Do you hurt anywhere?"

She smiled slightly and opened her eyes. "Other than my usual afflictions, no." She struggled to sit up. Cecilia rushed to help her.

"Don't try to stand; you need to sit here awhile. . . George, would you please bring over that pillow from the wing chair? We'll put it behind her back to make her more comfortable."

The vicar came in the door, followed by James.

"Is Lady Inglewood all right?" the vicar asked.

"I'm fine," Lady Inglewood assured him from her seat on the sofa.

He crossed the room and took her hands in his. "Dr. Patterson does not know if Squire Inglewood will live. He thinks the knife nicked a liver artery."

Lady Inglewood shrugged. "If I am arrested for murder, so be it."

"You won't be," James said, coming forward, "no matter the outcome. You were acting in the defense of others."

"I shudder to consider what you have suffered at the hands of that man," Cecilia said.

"It has only been in the last five years that he has become obsessed with respect, dignity, and power. He twists around a slight or disagreement into displaying disrespect, and that makes him livid. Only perfect agreement and obedience are accepted, and occasionally, even that can be twisted. It was like he looked for us and others to disrespect him. Expected it."

"But to hit you… How can you respect a man who does that?"

Lady Inglewood smiled slightly. "You learn."

"Mother, if he lives, you will not be safe living with him, you know that, don't you?" George said.

"Yes. But…I have a confession to make."

They looked at her quizzically.

"I followed my husband when he followed Mrs. Jones up on the downs. I haven't ridden a horse in years; however, I am a good rider. Better than Alfred."

"Which is the reason you haven't ridden in years," James said.

She smiled. "Yes… I kept to the line of trees at the far left side of the meadow. It was beautiful up there. The golden hour before dusk, when everything is bathed in warm golden light. I understood why Mrs. Jones liked to paint up there at that time of day.

"I saw him grab her around her neck to choke her. You were correct in your supposition that the pin came loose. It glinted in the sun and caught his hand. He sharply jerked that hand away. That gave Mrs. Jones the opportunity to run away from him. He chased her, cornering her near the cliff. She tried to get away, but he laughed at her. Laughed! …And he pushed her. I heard her scream, then nothing. I didn't consider that she might be alive. I rode back to Inglewood Manor quickly so he wouldn't know I had followed him."

"You saw him actually push her?" James clarified.

She nodded. "Strange, though, it appeared…slow and casual, and when she went down, he looked…satisfied."

"I do not blame you for not coming forward before now," the vicar told her. "But I don't understand why he wanted to claim she committed suicide."

"Even in death, he wanted to hurt her," Cecilia said.

Lady Inglewood agreed.

The vicar sadly nodded.

"If you are feeling up to standing now, you should go home and rest," Cecilia suggested.

"Yes, I'll fetch the carriage," George offered.

"Can you stand?" Cecilia asked.

"I think so."

She started to get up, then noticed the blood on her gown. "Oh, dear."

"Don't let it worry you."

"But the people outside?"

"All know what happened. Do not be embarrassed," Cecilia said.

Cecilia and James helped Lady Inglewood to her feet and led her outside. James lifted her into their carriage.

"Thank you," she murmured. Some people remained around the church, though many had gone home. Those who remained looked on her with sympathy.

James backed away.

"Oh! Sir James! Wait!" George said. He stuffed his hand in his pocket and pulled out a battered and creased letter. "I brought this with me to give you today and almost forgot!"

James took the letter from George Inglewood's outstretched hand and returned to Cecilia's side.

"The letter from your cousin?" Cecilia asked.

"It is his handwriting," James said.

Cecilia nodded. "Did the morning go as you expected?" she asked, threading her arm in his. They turned toward their home.

"Except for the knife and the gun, yes," he said.

"I never thought gossip could be useful in catching a criminal," she said as they walked the short distance to Summerworth Park.

"In many ways, anti-climactic," he said, his brow furrowing as he thought over the past week.

"Except for the knife and the gun," she parroted back.

He laughed.

EPILOGUE

THE LETTER

Cecilia sat in the nursery, nursing Hugh and telling Mary Alice what had happened that morning in church.

"When I was little, I remember Lady Inglewood as a smiling, laughing woman with a kind word for everyone. On holidays, she had treats for the village children, sweets she'd ordered all the way from London," Mary Alice said, her expression far away with her memories. "Back then, Squire was away from home for weeks at a time." Her face screwed up as she thought. "I don't remember why. Of course, as young as I was, I might not have known or cared," she said with a little laugh.

Hugh had fallen asleep while nursing. Cecilia shifted him to her shoulder and gently patted his back. She smiled as he scarcely woke when he burped. She laid him down in his bed.

"I am famished," she whispered to Mary Alice. "Have you eaten?"

"Yes, my lady."

Cecilia nodded, then quietly let herself out of the nursery.

She started downstairs but stopped when she saw James coming up.

"I was coming to find you," James said.

"I regret I cannot say the same. I am coming down to find food," she told him. "I am famished!"

"Heaven forfend that I stand in the way of my tiny wife when she is hungry," James declared, stepping aside with a gallant sweep of his body for her to go before him.

She playfully swatted at his arm.

"I will join you," he said, sobering. "I was coming to tell you of my cousin's letter. It is not like his previous missives."

She looked at him quizzically. "Is something wrong?"

"Yes, but we'll discuss it over food."

Her lips quirked, but she picked up her pace, her curiosity aroused.

Once they each had a plate of food and Daniel had served them beverages, James requested that Daniel leave the room and close the door behind him.

"Gracious!" Cecilia declared, surprised he'd asked Daniel to leave.

"You'll understand in a moment. Let's eat. Once we begin discussing my cousin's concerns, that will consume our time."

When they had finished, James pushed his plate away and leaned his elbows on the table. "The letter that George Inglewood has had for the past three days?"

"Yes?"

"As I said, it is from my cousin, Gideon Tallevast."

"The current Duke of Monteith," Cecelia said.

"Yes. He believes someone is either trying to injure him, drive him mad, or kill him."

"What?" Cecelia blinked at her husband, shocked. This was

nothing of what she expected to hear. "I know I have never met your cousin; however, from what you have told me, and what Mr. Thornbridge has relayed about how seriously he approaches the work to repair the Monteith fortunes, I would not take him for a man suffering flights of fancy."

"Gideon is not. He asks that we come to Devon to investigate. And to show you how worried he is, he sent his daughter, Chelsea, to my parents in Yorkshire. She doesn't know anything about what is going on, only that she is to spend the summer with her Great Aunt and Uncle Branstoke. He asks— if Miss Jones wishes to return to his employ as Chelsea's governess—that we send her to Yorkshire, as well."

Cecilia's brows drew together as she thought over what her husband told her. With danger inherent in the journey, her mother's protectiveness roared. She did not want to take Hugh. And she certainly did not want James to go by himself.

"Cecilia?" James said into a growing silence.

She waved a hand to request he wait. James's brow rose in amusement.

"The Aldriches," she finally said.

"The Aldriches?" James inquired.

"Yes. I'll ask Elinor and Simon if Mary Alice, her son, and Hugh might stay with them while we are gone. Ronnie and Charlotte are near enough in age to be playmates, which might be beneficial for both."

James nodded.

"We will take Sarah and your valet—they've both proven useful in the past. And I think we should take Mr. Romley."

James leaned back in his chair and laughed lightly. "I should have known my beautiful wife was planning military-style logistics. Anything else?"

"I have only started! Oh! I know, we will ask Mortlake for passage on his yacht. I must go upstairs and change for this afternoon. We need to speak with Mortlake, Miss Jones, and the Aldriches. …I rather hope Miss Jones decides to remain here while her charge is in Yorkshire. That would ease the vicar's grief to have at least one of his daughters near," Cecilia said as she rose from the table. She frowned for a moment. "I suppose we should also check on the condition of Squire Inglewood and make arrangements for Lady Inglewood to stay with someone for a few days. I don't think she should be by herself."

"Won't her son be with her?" James asked, rising as well.

"No, he'll be captaining the yacht, of course," she said off-handedly.

At that, James started to laugh.

"What?" Cecilia asked, looking at him crossly.

He shook his head. "Just you, my love. Just you." He pulled her toward him for a kiss. Then stepped away. "I'll have Romley bring the carriage around for this afternoon."

The end, until...
Murder with Apples

SCRIBBLINGS BY HOLLY NEWMAN

A Chance Inquiry series

Murder In Trade

Murder in Gold

Murder with Lilies

Murder of a Dead Man

Murder on the Downs

The Art of Love series

An Artful Deceit

An Artful Compromise

An Artful Lie

An Artful Secret

An Artful Decision

An Artful Practice

Flowers and Thorns series

A Grand Gesture

Honor's Players

A Heart in Jeopardy

Heart's Companion

Other works

Gentleman's Trade

Reckless Hearts

A Lady Follows

The Rocking Horse (novella)

Perchance to Dream (short story)

I live in Bradenton, Florida, with my husband and five cats. We moved here in 2019 ago after I spent 30 years in Phoenix, Arizona. I moved from one hot spot to another, but this location has rain and water.

Like many authors, I decided I wanted to write at a young age, and I filled notebook upon notebook with stories. However, in middle school, I had an English teacher tell me I did not have a writing talent, not like some of my classmates. My mother was furious, but the damage was done, my confidence was destroyed, and I stopped writing except for what I needed to write for classes.

Sometime later, after college, I started playing around with stories again. I couldn't find anything I wanted to read, so I wrote for myself. About this time, I went to a Science Fiction and Fantasy Convention with my then-boyfriend and there I met some authors.

Real live authors who were people like me!

Granted, these authors wrote Science Fiction, not Romance; however, they encouraged others to write and gave writing, plotting, and world-building workshops at Science Fiction and Fantasy conventions. As odd as it may sound, I can confidently say that I am a published author today because I learned that authors could be anybody and everybody.

If you want to write, pick up a pen or sit down at a computer and let the words come.

A small press bound by the belief that every voice matters.

Sign up for our newsletter to learn about new releases and more.
https://oliver-heberbooks.com/subscribe/

Follow us on social media:

facebook.com/oliverheberbooks
instagram.com/oliverheberbooks
amazon.com/oliverheberbooks
youtube.com/@OliverHeberBooksPublisher